Kirei
The Torihada Files

Tara A. Devlin

Kirei (The Torihada Files Book 3)
First Edition: July 2019
Illustrations by: Emiru the Yurei
http://www.instagram.com/emiru_1860/

taraadevlin.com
© 2019 Tara A. Devlin

DEDICATION

To all the crazy stuff you see in the big cities of the Japan, and the urban legends that helped inspire this story. And you, the readers, who stick with my work. Thank you.

CONTENTS

kirei [key-ray] *noun*
1. beautiful, lovely, pretty
    2. clean, clear, pure

1

"HEY, STOP, WHAT ARE YOU doing?"

A man removed my portrait from the top of the monthly leader boards and dropped it to the floor. He slotted a newer, smaller picture into second place—crooked—before replacing it with a face that made my blood boil; Noda Haruki. The up-and-coming hotshot of Rakucho's bustling host population.

"Are you kidding me right now?"

A rough pat on my shoulder made me turn around. I was greeted with the pompous man in the flesh. Disgust painted my face before I could stop it.

"What, not going to congratulate me?"

I could say nothing. If I opened my mouth, I feared the words that came out would end with one of us in hospital, and considering he was a good head higher than me and wider in the shoulder as well, it wasn't going to be him. Not to mention he was 15 years younger.

"Speechless, huh? It's okay, old man, I get it. I really do." He removed his hand from my shoulder and I rolled them back, trying to get rid of the slimy feeling running throughout my body. "You've been the number one host here at Club Tenshi for... how long now?"

"Two years." My voice cracked, and he smiled.

"Ah yes, two years. Since before I even started here, correct?"

I clenched my jaw. He grinned and looked up at the new monthly leader board. How I wished to punch that stupid smile off his face and then bend his portrait over his head.

"It was a good run, old man. I gotta give it to you. Even at... how old are you now? 40? 50?"

"36," I corrected him through gritted teeth. He smiled again and slapped his forehead.

"36, of course, how silly of me. Just looking at you, I thought, well... Anyway, it doesn't matter. Even at 36, you were still the number one host not only here, in our illustrious Club Tenshi, but in all of Rakucho! Or so they tell me."

It was true. For the last few years I had been the number one host at Club Tenshi, the most popular host club in Rakucho. When women wanted to have a good time, they came to see me. When women wanted to relieve the burden in their hearts, when they wanted someone to listen, when they wanted to drink and forget about the horrors of the real world, they came to see me, and I indulged them; for a price, of course. A man has to earn a living, and I made a damn good one. I started working as a host at 16, and I had the longest working history of any left in Rakucho. I saw generations come and go and no-one could touch my fame, my power, my wealth. Until this smug upstart.

"They tell you right. I'm assuming you can't read, otherwise you would know that for a fact from the *Host Monthly* magazine that's delivered right to our doorstep."

At that he laughed and sat down on a nearby stool, looking up to admire his own face. Lights glittered around the photo. The number one slot for the month was always larger than the others, which made it rather easy to keep once obtained. Once someone started their descent back down the ladder, that was it. Game over. People had been asking me for months whether I was going to retire while I was still at the top. Most hosts never lasted as long as I did, due to a variety of reasons, but I was no normal host. I was Shinji Narumi, the top host of Rakucho! One of the best hosts that ever lived! Why should I retire when I was still at the peak of my game? I could go on forever as number one!

Only now I wasn't. I was unceremoniously dumped on the floor, my photo lying in the dust as the old man on the ladder replaced me—crooked—with a newer, much smaller photo. Nobody coming to the club would see me now. They always picked number one, and if he was unavailable, only then might they start going down the line. Maybe. Or they might just come inside, have a drink with the cheapest guy available, and then head to the next bar to spend some time with *their* number one.

"Does this face look like it has time to read?" Haruki's words drew me back from my thoughts.

His eyebrows were raised, and he turned his head from side to side, showing off his profile.

"Women like someone who can have a conversation with them, you know, not just a caveman who cares more about his looks than they do."

He laughed, loudly and uproariously. He slapped the wooden bar a few times and stood up. "I like you." He pointed at me, leaning down to my height. "I can see why you were number one for so long. I get it now, I do. You're a funny guy. I mean, your hairstyle's a little out of date, sure, and those boots haven't been in fashion for years, but... you're funny. I get it. I'm sure there are lots of older women out there who still like that sorta thing. You probably remind them of their youth, when—" he took a step back and motioned his hands in the air "—all of this was still in vogue, I guess. But the young girls, the pretty girls, well..." He turned and looked up his photo again and smiled. "They're after something a little more modern, if you know what I mean. They don't care what I have to say, just as much as I don't care what they have to say. You really don't think all of these women come to see us because we give them stimulating conversation?" He pressed his lips together and tried to suppress a laugh. "You poor old man. No, they want something else stimulated. And I'll have you know that I'm very, very good at that, if you catch my drift..."

He let the words hang in the air a moment, his eyes locked on mine. It took everything I had not to leap forward, put my hands around his neck, and then beat that stupid look off his face. Let's see how much the women like your "stimulation" when you don't have that pretty face to back it up. But even if beating his face didn't get me fired—the boss was a friend of mine from way back—it would get me sent home for the evening, and it would lead to further tensions with Haruki down the line that would end in one of us getting the sack. I had a lifestyle to maintain. I couldn't afford that.

So, I grinned. I forced myself to smile and clenched my jaw closed so the poison sitting on the end of my tongue didn't escape of its own accord and make matters worse. He was just an upstart. He took first place this month, so what? Women liked a reliable man, an attentive man, and Haruki was neither of those things. He was a pretty face with a silk tongue and a bit of luck. Next month I'd be back at the top of the leader boards and everything would go back to normal.

Everything would be just fine.

2

MY HEAD ACHED. IT TOOK me a few moments to realise where I was; at home, in my own bed. Something warm and firm pressed against me. I rolled over and my head pounded even more. Bits and pieces of the night slowly came back to me. Haruki taking my first spot on the leader board. A party of women arriving with more money than wits to spend. Haruki taking all of them. A lone office lady who requested Haruki, but he was too busy with the large party of women to be able to give his undivided attention to her, so she settled for me instead. And here we were. Naked and me with a throbbing headache.

I crawled out of bed and fumbled around in the nearby dresser for some pills. I chewed them straight and stumbled over to the sink for a drink. Coughs racked my body and the pain in my head exploded into bright lights.

"Ugh."

When I was in my teens and early 20s, I could drink for days and feel no signs of pain or sickness. Iron Shinji they called me, for my iron stomach and iron lungs. Several packs of cigarettes a day on top of the near constant drinking required to reach the top level of my chosen profession. A profession I cared deeply about. Not like that shithead Haruki. Just because he came into the world with a pretty face, he thought he knew how to entertain a woman? He knew nothing.

I straightened up and several bones cracked. My knees ached and there was an odd pain in my left shoulder that had been building for several months. Now when I drank, I was left with a hangover for several days unless I started drinking more to forget about it. Another series of coughs racked my body, like a lung was trying to escape its prison, and my vision blurred as I leaned against the counter.

"You okay?" A sleepy voice from the bed called out. What was her name again?

"Fine. Smoker's cough. You know?" If smoker's cough was a lung trying to eject itself from a body because it had had enough.

"Not really, no," she said. "What time is it?"

Harsh light poured in through the curtain. "I dunno, the clock is there."

Suddenly she jumped up and started grabbing her clothes. "Oh shit, I need to be at work in 20 minutes!"

I swallowed more precious water. She darted around the room in a haze. I stopped trying to follow her and closed my eyes. This was what being hit by a truck felt like, wasn't it? And it was only getting worse. Maybe they were right. Maybe I was getting on in years and several decades of abuse was wearing my body down. Or maybe I just needed another drink.

"Where are my cigarettes…?" I stuck my hand down the back of the couch. I could have sworn I threw them there on the way to the bedroom. I remembered at least that much. The girl—what was her name?—wasn't unpleasant when she was introduced to me, but she was clearly hoping for Haruki. Still, I knew my way around a woman and before long she was laughing and telling me her life story, her hopes and goals, her pains and problems. That's all they really wanted, you know, just someone to listen. They didn't want a douchebag jumping in with tales about the time he had to fend off ten women at once, or how he went out with his mates and came home with several days' worth of memories missing. That didn't impress women, and Haruki would learn that soon enough. Learn it the hard way, no doubt.

Things went so well that she agreed to join me for drinks after the club closed. Of course, the clubs in Rakucho were the last things to close, so that meant back at my place. She jumped at the chance… Or, I thought she did. Parts of it were hazy. But I did remember her shoving me into the door, ripping my belt off, throwing my cigarettes on the couch so they wouldn't get crushed underfoot, and then falling into bed.

Then it was daylight, and my head was pounding. Another drink would fix that. "Have you seen my cigarettes?" I asked, lifting the cushions.

"Have I what? No. Were you even listening to me just now?"

I scratched my head and squinted, trying to make out her face. "Yes."

"What did I just say?" She planted her hands on her hips. She was not happy.

"That you need to get to work."

"I said that several minutes ago."

I swallowed. My throat felt like a porcupine was using it as its own private race tunnel. "I'm sorry, it's early and I just... I need my smokes."

She held a packet up before my nose. "They were on your bedside, genius."

I grabbed them and lit one up, allowing the smoke to spread throughout my lungs and sighing in bliss. "You're a doll."

"I was saying, while you were looking for the cigarettes that were right there on your bedside table, that I need to get to work, and could you possibly give me a lift?"

The pounding in my head throbbed harder and faster. My stomach churned.

"I don't..." I fought to keep whatever was in my stomach down "...have a car..."

"You don't have a car?" She scoffed. "That's just wonderful. Could you at least call a cab?"

I pointed to the land line phone that I never used. "Phone's there. You can put it on my tab."

She put her hands on her hips again.

"What?"

"Are you serious?"

"About?"

"You're not even going to call me a cab?"

"Are you unable to use a phone?"

She scoffed again, unable to hide her disgust.

"You're a real gentleman, you know. A real fucking pro." She walked over to the phone and picked it up.

"Why am I the one at fault here? You didn't even pick me in the first place! You picked that other fuckface!"

She raised an eyebrow and spoke to the person on the other end of the line, her eyes boring into me. When she was done, she hung up and grabbed her things.

"You're a real piece of work, Shinji Narumi. And yes, I know your name. I'll make sure not to ask for you next time. You clearly have no idea of how to treat a woman."

"What? Hey, come on! What did I even do?" She slammed the door behind her on her way out. The bang was like a hammer crashing into my skull. Whatever. She was just one woman. You couldn't win them all, and her day might have just been starting, but mine wasn't. I crawled back into bed.

3

IT WAS DARK OUTSIDE WHEN I woke again. I fumbled for my phone, knocking it off the bedside table to the floor.

"Dammit."

It was past 8 p.m. I still had an hour or so before I needed to be out the door and at work.

"Man, I could have had another hour of sleep." The continued pounding in my head suggested that it would have been a good idea, too. I grabbed a few more painkillers and washed them down with an open beer from the fridge.

"Ugh, oh god, how long has that been in there?" Tiny pinpricks of bitter staleness stabbed my tongue and clawed for life all the way down my throat. I poured the rest of the drink down the sink and opened a fresh one. No good going to work sober. Then I had to not only sit through Haruki's stupid face, but my headache as well. One of those things I had to deal with, but if I could avoid the other, I would.

Coughs wracked my body as I lit another cigarette. Cars sped by beneath the window as I stopped to look outside. With all the hustle and bustle of Rakucho, it was one of my favourite things to do before work. A small moment of quiet "me" time. No women to impress, no money to make, no assholes to ignore. Just me, a drink, a cigarette, and the world flying by outside without me. It was like I had stepped outside of time itself. I was my own separate entity watching humanity move about like ants, and I, a god. Nobody knew I was there, watching them. Sometimes I imagined lives for those passing by. That guy was a businessman who lost a big contract last week and now he's wondering whether he's ever going to get that promotion. Ha, thank god that's not me. That woman down there walking with two kids, she just broke up with her deadbeat baby daddy and now she's taking the kids to see grandma while she works nights so they don't starve. Thank god I didn't have kids, phew. Dodged that bullet.

Every person down there had a story. I had no idea who they were, and they had no idea who I was. But I could see them, and they couldn't see me, so that gave me the upper hand. Once I saw a man attacking a woman from my window before work. She was standing by the bus stop, minding her own business, when a man ran past and grabbed her bag. She screamed and chased after him, but then he turned a corner and was gone. Did she ever get her bag back? Probably not. Could I have done anything from my window? Maybe yelled out for him to stop? Caught his attention long enough for her to catch up to him and grab her bag back? Maybe, but unlikely. Nothing I did would have made a real difference, and that was life, wasn't it? Everyone went about their lives doing their own thing, only barely interacting with others to the absolute minimum needed to get through their day.

I opened my phone. Several messages popped up.

"You're a real dick, you know? You don't even have a tab. I had to pay for the taxi myself! And I was late to work! I thought you might have been different. You're older than the others, and I'm not into old guys but I thought, hey, might as well try it once, maybe he'll surprise you. You didn't surprise me, Narumi. In fact, you were not only the worst I've ever had, but you're a real pig of a man, too. For someone who spent all night talking about himself, you really are clueless, aren't you?"

I took another swig of my drink and let the words sink in. Me? A pig? Clueless? What on earth was she on about? I didn't get to be the number one host in Rakucho by talking about myself all night! And the worst she ever had? That was just uncalled for! I tried to remember the night before, but after hitting the bed, everything was blank. Sure, maybe in my drunken state I wasn't in much condition to satisfy a woman, but she knew that when she came back with me. Now, granted, in my younger days that much alcohol would have been a starter for me, but...

...I didn't know where that line of thought was going. My cheeks flushed hot with rage and I flicked the cigarette butt out the window.

"Just who the hell does she think she is? She's not into 'older guys'? What the hell does that even mean? Does she think she's some hot stuff too good for the rest of us? What the fuck?"

I threw my work clothes on and jumped into a cab. I got out at the usual hairdresser and swore at her all about the ungrateful woman in my life as she did my hair, then went downstairs to the convenience store. Cigarettes. I needed more. Maybe some beer, too.

"Sir, your card has been declined."

I grabbed a stick of gum from the candy beside the register and blinked a few times. "I'm sorry, what?"

He turned the pin machine around to face me. "There's no money in this card, sir."

I rifled through my pockets and put a few notes down on the counter. "Here, is this enough?"

The cashier took two bills and pushed the rest back towards me. I stuffed them into my back pocket and smiled, holding the cigarette box up in thanks.

"Thank you for shopping at Family Cart."

His voice was as dead as my energy levels. I cracked a can and downed it before I hit the corner, tossing it into the trash. Alright. Work clothes on, hair done, alcohol and cigarettes in me... The card I could deal with at another time, it was probably just their fuck up, and I was early for work. How's that, Haruki? I bet your immature ass still doesn't get to work on time, number one or not. Women love a reliable man. You gotta give them something stable or they won't come back.

"Hey! Watch where you're going, geezer!" A young thug in all green clothes shoved me against the wall. "We're standing here, ya know?"

I brushed my shirt. No point getting dirty before work. "Yes, I can see that, punk." The kids laughed. They couldn't have been out of their teens, and they all wore green from head to toe. "A colour gang? Really? And they say I'm the one who's out of touch."

"What's that, old man?" One of the kids pressed himself up in my face. He would have been more intimidating if he had another 10 years and 10 kilos on him.

"I said, that's very brave of you children to go outside wearing colour coordinated clothes so you don't lose each other in the big bad crowds. Did your mummy pick those colours for you? I mean, the green does stand out nicely in a crowd, so if you ever lose her hand I'm sure she can still spot you a mile away."

He slammed his fist into the wall beside my head.

"You speak big for a man about to taste pavement."

"I've tasted pavement before. It's not very nice. Have you?"

The kids behind him laughed. "Leave him be. If you hit him he'd probably break, it's not even worth it."

My head pounded from the impact against the wall and the alcohol running through my veins, but I couldn't let him know that.

"I tell ya what, old man, you do look kinda feeble, so I'd hate to have to carry ya to the hospital. How about you pay us a small restitution fee and we'll be on our way. We'll forget this whole thing ever happened."

"Restitution. That's a big word for a special boy like you. Did your mummy teach you that one too?"

He grabbed my shirt and yanked me close. His breath stank of alcohol and tiny red veins ran wild through his eyes. He was what I would have been if I hadn't picked up my first hosting job after running away from home. Part of me felt bad for him, but another, more pressing part, wanted to kick him in the nuts and teach him a lesson about picking on people in public.

"You're going to pay us or we're going to fuck you up, you hear me?"

I turned my face to the side and waved a hand in front of my nose. "You kiss your mother with that mouth? Ever heard of mouthwash? Geez…"

He shook me again and one of his buddies placed a hand on his shoulder. "Yo, just leave him be. A crowd's gathering and we got places to be, man."

"You hear that? Mummy's calling. Better get going." The youth in green let go of me and adjusted the sweater he was wearing. "Go on, wouldn't want to keep her waiting."

He stuck a finger in my face and leaned in close. "If I see you again, you better be ready to pay up. You're lucky we have business elsewhere right now."

I brushed his finger away from my face and ran a

hand through my hair. I just got that how I liked it, dammit. "And you better get out of my face before I decide that you need the spanking your mother clearly never gave you."

The kids moved on, the leader keeping an eye on me as his friends dragged him away. I fixed my shirt, checked my hair was still set, and made my way down the main street of Rakucho. All eyes were on me after that little scene and I knew it. I stopped before the sign at the end of the street that advertised Club Tenshi's hosts. We had the biggest sign in town, and in the best location as well. Anyone coming in or out of Rakucho would see it, and there I was, front and centre, a veritable Prince Charming ready to make a lady or ladies forget about all their worries. That was what they paid me for, after all, and I was the best. Screw whatever the monthly leader board said. I was the number one host, not Haruki.

A figure out the corner of my eye caught my attention. The streets were filling with people as Rakucho's night life kicked into high gear, but there was something odd about her. Was it a her? She was too far away to tell. I tilted my head. A trench coat and face mask? In the middle of summer? I blinked, and she was gone. I shook my head and shrugged. Not the oddest thing I'd ever seen in Rakucho, but still. It would have to wait until another time though. My patrons were waiting for me.

4

WHAT A DRAG.

Haruki sat in the middle of a bench surrounded by women. A few of the newer hosts hung around on the outskirts, hoping to squeeze their way in and maybe earn a few favours with the women who were unable to reach Haruki directly. Leeches. They were all leeches. Every single one of them.

"So then I tell the guy, 'Listen, you're gonna have to try a little harder than that if you're trying to scare me.' I mean, look at me!" Haruki's voice boomed across the noisy club. He held his arm up and flexed, allowing several women to touch and poke it while they oohed and aahed. They giggled, and he pushed more glasses of champagne towards them. "But enough about me, drink! Drink! Tonight is all about you ladies, and I am all about pleasing the ladies after all, if you catch my drift..."

I fought the urge to vomit. A noise at the entrance caught my attention and my face lit up.

One of my regulars! Finally, I could show them how a pro went to work. I slicked my hair back, put my cigarette out, and sidled over to her.

"Good evening, ma'am."

"Hi, yeah, is Haruki available?" Her eyes scanned the dark room, ignoring me completely. I coughed to clear my throat.

"Hey, it's me!"

She turned to look at me for a moment, as though finally registering who I was, and then went back to scanning the dark room. "Yeah, hi. So, is he free? Haruki?"

I opened my mouth a few times, but the words refused to come out. Instead of "Hello, I'm standing right here, we drank together last week!" a choked sound caught in the back of my throat.

"I, uh, no, he's busy."

"When will he be free?"

"I don't know."

"Can you find someone that does?"

Did she even know who I was? It was dark, maybe she hadn't seen me and confused me for the door staff. I placed a hand on her arm and leaned down into the light so she could see me better.

"I can take care of you, ma'am. Haruki is otherwise engaged and would make for poor company right now. If you come this way, then—"

She pulled herself free from my grip and grabbed her phone. "Can I book some time with him?"

I gritted my teeth. "I don't know, ma'am. I'm not the door staff."

"Oh? Well, who are you then? Can you get someone who can help me?"

I could almost see the smoke rising from my skin. Who are you? What type of question was that? It took all I had to stop from grabbing her and shaking her several times until the fog clouding her vision lifted and she saw the number one host of Rakucho standing right in front of her. Who was I? Only the most important man she would see that night!

It was no use. Her eyes were fixated on anything but me, and to be honest, after that treatment I wasn't sure that I wanted to spend time with her anyway. It was a two-way street. The ladies picked us as much as we picked them. That was how a good host did it. How could you get a lady to open up and spend her money if you had nothing in common? If you didn't even want to be around her? It went both ways, and my insides were burning at the slight.

"Please wait here," I mumbled and walked over to the bar. I told the bartender Koji about her problem and he walked over to deal with her. What a shit show.

More women filed in as the night went on. I forgot about the woman from earlier as several regulars came in to fill me in on their days, share a drink and a laugh, and otherwise enjoy some good company. Just like old times. Except unlike old times, the gaps between customers were getting larger and larger. Just a few short months ago my schedule was packed from opening till closing, and often after as well. That was when real hosts made their best money. Not all business had to be conducted inside, and often the real profit came not from the money, but from the gifts the women gave you in private. A new car. A new watch. A new TV. A trip to some exotic location. A good host never had to pay for anything new again, and his direct earnings from the club could pile nicely in the bank until he was ready to retire.

Retire. The word left a bad taste in my mouth. I would retire on my own terms when I was ready. No sooner, no later. There were still a few good years left in me.

An image flashed at the door and my heart jumped. A trench coat? I got out of my chair and ran over to the door, but by the time I got there, she was gone.

"Hey, Koji, did you see that woman? Where did she go?"

The bartender looked up from the glass he was drying. "What woman?"

"Right here. There was a woman in a trench coat."

He shook his head. "I didn't see anyone."

Something about her creeped me out. The way she looked at me earlier when I saw her in the distance. It was like time slowed down and everyone else was moving, but her focus was solely on me, even through the giant crowds. She had to be a customer, or at the very least, a potential customer. Perhaps she recognised me from the sign, but either way, something about her made my skin crawl. Customers who turned into stalkers weren't uncommon, and the fact she hid her features under that trench coat and mask, even in the dead heat of summer, sent alarm bells ringing.

"Well, if you do see a woman in a trench coat, just play it safe, okay? I saw some woman watching me today and better safe than sorry, you know?"

"Yeah, sure. Whatever you say, boss."

I smiled. Koji was a good guy and had been at the club nearly as long as I had. He always had my back.

"Oh, by the way, one of your regulars came down before while you were with the customer from the law firm."

"Oh yeah? Is she waiting somewhere?"

Koji grimaced and shook his head. "She said she wanted to 'try something new' tonight." He jerked his chin, and I turned. She was sitting with several other women beside Haruki. Again his laughter bellowed throughout the club, quite an achievement considering the volume of the music. "Thought you might want to know."

I took a deep breath and held it in my chest a moment before letting it out. So that was how it was going to be, huh?

"Thanks for telling me."

"Don't take this the wrong way or anything..." Koji put a glass down and planted his hands firmly on the bench "...but have you ever seriously considered retiring?" There it was, that word again. Retiring. All around me, like a leftover piece of cake that nobody wanted anymore; not because it was mouldy, but because it had been out in the open the longest and the edges had gone slightly hard and the colours faded.

"Not you too..."

"I'm just saying, you're the best man I've ever

known to work this job, but no man sustains the same work forever. You're better than this. You could do anything you want with the money you've made here over the last 20 years, hell, I wouldn't be surprised if you could buy every single host club in town. That's the goal, isn't it?"

"What? Buying out all the other clubs?"

"Not necessarily, but, you know, moving on. Into management or something. A job where you don't have to be 'on' all night, where you don't have to smoke and drink until the small hours of the morning each and every day, a job where you don't have to constantly keep at the height of fashion and hairstyles and make up, yeah? And I can only imagine how it feels to have the same conversations with people over and over, I mean, that sounds like my idea of hell…"

I grabbed a can from behind the counter and poured it into a glass.

"I like all of that," I said, taking a swig. "These women don't just come here to spend money. They have money, yes, but if they just wanted to spend it on some man, then they could pick up an escort somewhere and be done with it. That's not what this is about, Koji. You know that. We provide a unique service. Not just a shoulder to cry on, but a friend, someone who can truly listen, someone who can offer real advice, someone who can make them laugh and forget about their troubles. We all have troubles, Koji, and it's our job to help them with that on top of everything else. This is the only place in the world where they can get all of those things together."

Koji fell silent for a moment. "I don't know how you do it, Narumi. After 20 years, how are you not tired? How is your body not breaking down?"

I grinned. Well, some things couldn't be avoided, but nobody else had to know that.

"These women need me. Look at Haruki. Look at him." I screwed my face up. "He's a punk. He was blessed with good looks at birth and hasn't got a single working brain cell in his head. He's good looking, but it takes more than that to be a top host. People will soon realise he's all show and no substance. We all have rough months, Koji. This is mine. They'll be back when they realise Haruki doesn't have what they're looking for, and it's my duty to take care of them."

"Big words, Narumi."

"But true."

"Maybe. You're a crazier man than I."

"Ain't that the truth."

We shared a smile, and a woman came running down the stairs, barrelling directly into my back. For a moment I panicked, thinking it was the woman in the trench coat, but it was another face. What was her name again?

"You asshole!" She swung her arms wildly, battering me around the face and shoulders. "You fucking asshole!"

Koji ran out from behind the counter and attempted to restrain the woman. "Hey, whoa, none of that in here."

"Let go of me, pervert!" She swung her arms and extracted herself from Koji's grip. "Don't touch me! And you! You're a piece of shit!"

It was the woman from the night before. Satoko? Satomi? Sahomi? It was something like that.

"Look, Satoko—"

"It's Miku!"

Okay, it was nothing like that.

"…Miku, listen. Let's sit down and have a drink. Let's talk about—"

"You took me home and treated me like crap, not to mention whatever the hell it was you did before passing out, because it certainly wasn't sex, and then you made me call my own taxi and guess what, they didn't have a tab. I had to pay for the whole thing myself! I had the money, that wasn't the problem." She thrust a finger into my chest. "You. You're the problem, you piece of shit. After all the chatting and drinking and pretending to listen and be my friend, you're just as bad as the others."

Several eyes in the club turned our way. Everyone loved a good argument.

"You whisper sweet nothings and act all high and mighty, when in reality you're just a dog. I honestly thought you might be different. I mean, you don't exactly have your looks going for you anymore, do you? And you're not good in the sack, so I dunno what it was that made you so popular, but it had to be your personality, right?"

A few women nearby giggled. I straightened up and puffed out my chest.

"But your personality is even uglier than your face. I won't be coming back here again, don't worry, but I wanted you to know why. You're a piece of shit. Maybe they can't see it, but I can."

She brushed past Koji and stomped up the stairs.

Haruki stifled a giggle and poured another drink for one of his customers. "Well, that was embarrassing…"

"Why don't you take the rest of the night off?" Koji suggested. I shrugged him off.

"She's the crazy one, not me. The night's still young and I've still got work to do." Several coughs racked my body. I lit up another cigarette. Sometimes you just couldn't reach a person no matter how hard you tried. "And not my fault she called the wrong taxi company, geez…"

5

TRY AS I MIGHT, I couldn't get that woman's words out of my head. It soured the rest of the evening, and in the end I went home alone and tired. Not the usual kind of tired from a long night of drinking and partying, but the type of tired from spending all night running around inside my head. No matter how I looked at it, I couldn't reconcile the woman's words with who I really was. I wasn't the one at fault. Could I have treated her better? Perhaps. I wasn't perfect, but I knew how to treat a woman, and I most certainly wouldn't try to shame her in front of her colleagues. That was the part that hurt the most. She did it at my place of business. In front of colleagues and customers. They were all talking about it. I knew they were. That was all it took for unfounded rumours to start. I needed to nip it in the bud before it got out of control. I wasn't at fault here. She was.

When I stepped through the smoky haze

lingering in front of Club Tenshi's entrance, my worst fears were confirmed. People were whispering to each other in all corners of the club. They looked up and fell silent as I stepped through the door before returning to their whispered silver-tongued lies. "He doesn't know how to treat a woman," they were no doubt whispering. "You need to watch out for him, he doesn't care, he just wants your money." I didn't even know how much money I had. It wasn't a concern of mine. I lived the life my customers afforded me. Nothing more, nothing less. Sure, my credit card was declined the day before, but it wasn't like that was an uncommon occurrence. That happened to everyone. Money was the least of my concerns. The health and well-being of my customers came first. Why couldn't they see that?

Two of the newer hosts fell silent as I walked up to them. They looked everywhere but at me.

"What?" I said.

"Hmm? Sorry? What's that?" The youngest straightened as stiff as a rod. What was his name? Jin? Jo?

"What were you whispering about?"

"Oh, no, we weren't, it's just—"

Koji threw a newspaper down in front of me. He looked at the hosts and they took the opportunity to run, blending into the wallpaper as best they could.

"They were talking about this."

I picked the paper up and gave Koji a suspicious look. "What am I supposed to be looking at?"

He pointed to the headline. There was a picture beneath it of police tape with a familiar sign in the background. "This."

Host Killed in Rakucho the headline read. I scanned through the article and put the newspaper back down. Koji's eyebrows were raised. "It's been a while."

"10 years, at least."

Rakucho was a dangerous place. Many called it the seedy side of the capital, but to me it was home. It wasn't seedy, it was different. It sat outside the strict norms of society so people naturally blamed it whenever something bad happened nearby. But a murder in Rakucho? Those were surprisingly rare, let alone of a host.

"Do we know who it was?"

Koji shook his head. "The boss has been on the phone since he got in, trying to find out. Rumour has it that it was one of Serenity's boys. A new guy, barely outta his teens."

I lit a cigarette and motioned for Koji to pour me a drink. "Do they know who did it? Or why?"

He pushed the drink towards me and shook his head again. "But everyone's pretty shaken up about it. The last time someone was murdered in Rakucho—"

"—it led to a gang war that saw numerous bars and clubs getting raided and closed down, and it didn't even have anything to do with us to begin with."

Koji nodded. "The boss is on edge. He doesn't want anything like last time to happen again. It took all the contacts and 'gifts' he had to keep this place running as the cops ran all over the place shutting things down. Not to mention it's not good for business in general. Scared people don't like to go out at night, let alone get drunk."

The beer burned as it went down. I followed it with another quick swig to keep the burgeoning cough down. "It's a little early to be worrying, isn't it? It's just one guy, and by the sounds of it, just a kid. Some kids hassled me on my way in the other day, it's probably just some young punks who fucked up and don't know any better."

Koji picked the paper up and hid it under the counter, out of sight. "Could be. I hope so. Anyway, the boss wants everyone on their best behaviour tonight." He paused and looked pointedly at me.

"What?"

"Even you, Narumi."

I laughed and spat up some of my drink. Koji wiped his cheek with disgust.

"When have I ever not been on my best behaviour?"

"The boss wasn't impressed with that little scene you made last night."

"I did no such thing! She was the one who came in here screaming untruths and—"

"The boss doesn't care. Whatever you do after hours is your own business, but you can't be bringing that shit in here. Especially not now."

"What's that supposed to mean?"

Koji looked around to see if anyone was nearby and leaned forward. "Look, the boss loves you like a brother, you two have a long history and—"

"—And?"

He sighed. "The fact is, you're not bringing in as much money as you used to. He's been talking about your retirement and looking for some new guys to take your place. You'll be happy to know that he's looking at several people. It's gonna be a big gap to fill."

I pushed myself out of the chair, sending it crashing to the ground. Koji took a step back.

"Big gap to fill? Retirement! You mean getting fired! Because that's what this is, isn't it?"

Koji held his hands up in the air. "I'm just relaying what I heard."

"That's why you were asking me about it last night, isn't it?"

"Narumi—"

"Not another word, Koji. I've had it up to here with all of this." I stormed over to one of the couches and sat down, splashing my drink all over the table. One of the younger hosts rushed over with a cloth to clean it up. I glared at him and he bowed and ran away like a dog with his tail between his legs. Retirement. That was all anybody could think about. Over and over, like a broken record.

"Naaaaaarumi."

The first syllable was drawn out in a sing-song voice. Haruki stood above me, a woman on either side.

"What?"

"You look upset."

His face wasn't making matters better.

"Did you hear about what happened to that host?" One of the women leaned forward, spilling some of her drink. Haruki laughed uproariously as it splashed on my boots. "How scary, right?" The other woman nodded in agreement. Come to think of it, the other woman looked familiar.

"Yuri, was it?"

The woman's eyebrows rose. "I'm sorry?"

"Your name. Yuri, right?"

The colour drained from her face when she realised who she was speaking to. Yes, Yuri. Another of my old regulars who had apparently now abandoned me for Haruki. She was in earlier than usual, perhaps hoping not to run into me. I grinned, keenly aware that the smile never left my lips. She dipped her head a few times and said nothing more. It was fine. She didn't need to say anything else.

"Narumi!" Koji's voice rang out over the music. "A customer!"

I pushed myself off the couch. "Well, would you look at that? Barely here a few minutes and already somebody is after me. If you'll excuse me."

I brushed past and heard the women whispering as I walked by. Just give it time. They would realise how little Haruki had to offer after spending time with him. It was their loss, not mine.

Several homely women stood beside Koji at the door. They appeared to be housewives in their late 40s or early 50s. I pasted the best grin I could on and bowed. "Good evening, ladies. My name is Narumi, and I hear that you fine women are looking for a good time, is that correct?" A few of them giggled while another clutched at her purse, unsure if she should be in such an establishment at this hour. "If you'll gladly follow me…"

Haruki's grin grew wider when he saw the troop of middle-aged women sit down. The women with him didn't bother to hide their amusement. It was emblazoned across their faces. "How the mighty have fallen." Work had barely even begun and already the mood had soured.

"Are you a host here?" One of the women said. I forced a smile.

"I am."

"Oh, I'm terribly sorry. I thought you were one of the staff…"

The woman next to her slapped her friend. I continued to force the smile.

"You can't just say that to people…" her friend said.

"What? He looks closer to our age than theirs." The woman looked over at Haruki and his bevy of women. I closed my eyes and let the music wash over me for a moment. The pain in my knees throbbed.

"I saw in the newspaper that a young man was murdered several streets away last night." The woman's friend quickly changed the subject. "Did you know him?"

"I can't say I did, no."

Koji placed a few buckets of champagne and bottles of beer on the table and disappeared from view.

"They say he was just a kid," she continued. "Poor thing."

"I wouldn't know." It was difficult to keep the grin going, and the murder was the last thing I wanted to talk about. "So, what brings you ladies here tonight? I don't believe I've seen you around before."

"Oh, Setsuko wanted to try something new."

They looked at the woman clutching her bag like her life savings were in it. "It's her birthday."

"Your birthday!" My voice came out louder and more enthusiastic than I intended. "Well, a special occasion calls for a special drink!"

"I don't drink," she muttered, looking at the ground.

"I'll have one!" one of her friends said.

"Me too!"

I popped the cork on the most expensive bottle there and poured drinks for everyone. Setsuko continued staring at the ground.

"I heard that the police already have a suspect. It wasn't in the papers, but my husband works close to the police station and he overheard the officers talking when they came in for lunch."

"No way!"

"A witness saw someone in a trench coat nearby…"

My ears perked up, and I placed a hand on the woman's arm. "I'm sorry, I didn't catch your name."

"Emiko."

"Emiko. What a beautiful name. What's this about a trench coat?"

It was her. It had to be.

6

LINES OF FACE MASKS STARED back at me from the convenience store shelves. There were not only different brands, but different types and different shapes as well. Masks that covered your whole face. Masks that covered your nose and cheeks. Masks for your forehead. Masks shaped like funny animals. Masks with patterns. Masks that moisturised and pulled out blackheads and all sorts of things I never knew a mask could do.

"I thought you were staff..."

Rich, coming from a woman in her 50s, but still. The words stung. They didn't consider me a hot young stud, they considered me an equal. I wasn't their equal, I was still close to 20 years younger than them. 20! All the kids were always talking about masks, so that seemed like a good place to start. At the very least, it couldn't hurt.

"Welcome." The cashier's voice rang out as the bell above the door tinkled and another customer walked in. I stuck my hands in my pockets and wandered over to the toilet. I locked the door behind me and carefully stepped over a puddle of I didn't want to know what. The bright lights above the mirror shone harsh light down upon me, highlighting the deep grooves in my face. I squinted and turned my head from side to side.

"I'm not that old…"

Not that you could tell. Perhaps the women were right. All those years of drinking and smoking hadn't been kind to my skin. Not like I had a healthy diet either. Breakfast was beer at around 4 or 5 in the afternoon. Lunch didn't exist, and dinner was whatever I grabbed on my way home in the small hours of the morning, usually something quick from the convenience store or, if I was on an after-hours date with one of the customers, a 24-hour yakiniku restaurant nearby.

Perhaps it was time to start taking better care of myself. A face mask or two couldn't hurt, and they weren't expensive either. I waited for the doorbell outside to tinkle, flushed the toilet and walked back out again. It wouldn't be very good for my image for people to see me buying cosmetics at this hour. This face was natural!

I grabbed a random selection of masks and threw them in a basket. Some vitamin drinks nearby called my name, so I threw a couple of those in and dropped the basket on the counter.

"Welcome," the cashier said in his monotone voice.

"Are these masks any good?"

He didn't look up from scanning. "I haven't used

them before, sir, but they are a popular product."

I fell silent and handed him my card. He scanned, and the machine beeped a few times.

"Sir, you've been declined." The flatness of his voice bored into my skull. Shit, I forgot to check why that card was being declined. I pulled out my wallet. A few sad bills looked back at me. I handed them to him and took the bag with a small nod.

"Thank you for shopping at Family Cart…"

I cracked open a drink and let the sweet vitamin-y flavour pour down my throat. Tasted like health. I'd call the bank in the morning when I woke up. There was no way I was out of money. I made a good living as the number one host of Rakucho. Maybe the card was damaged? Anyway, in the morning.

A figure bumped into me, pushing me back into the convenience store door. The glass in my hand fell to the street, its contents pouring out in the gutter.

"Hey, watch where you're goi—"

The word froze in my throat. A trench coat. A dark trench coat was disappearing down the street. I blinked a few times. No doubt about it.

"Hey!" I ran down the street, pushing through the crowds that were filing home as the final bars and clubs closed. "Get out of the way! Stop her!"

I looked down at my shirt. Blood. There was blood on it.

"Hey! Stop!"

I reached the end of the street, standing before the sign of myself smiling down. She was gone. To the right of me was empty, and a lone couple were walking down the left. I rubbed my fingers together and sniffed them. Metallic. It was her. Where did she go?

I ran back to the top of the street and hailed a taxi. It was Mitsuhiro, one of my usual drivers from the Blue Taxi company. He recognised me immediately.

"Home, sir?"

I nodded and hid the bloodstain on my shirt with the convenience store bag.

"You okay, sir?"

I nodded again and smiled. "Yeah, sure, perfectly fine. Why's that?"

"You seem a little shaken. Did something happen?" He pulled out leisurely into traffic and turned in the direction of my house. Mitsuhiro had been driving me home for years. He was a good man with three children of his own and never complained, not even that time when one of my dates threw up in the back of his cab. He told me to forget about it and cleaned the mess up himself. A real good man.

"Did you hear about the host that was murdered here last night?" I asked. His eyes lit up in the rear-view mirror.

"Oh, that! Yes, it's been the talk of the town all night. It's been a while since anything like that happened here, hasn't it?"

I nodded. "Do you know anything about it?"

Mitsuhiro shook his head and turned another corner. The meter ticked like gun shots to my head in the silence. He always did everything at his own pace, even conversations. "Nothing more than what

I saw in the news, sir."

"What did the news say?"

"The police were still looking for a suspect. Nobody seems to be quite sure of what really happened. The police haven't released any information, but another of the drivers said that a customer told him it was another host."

"Another host?" It couldn't be. That wouldn't make any sense. "Why would another host do something like that? It's bad for business. Nobody's gonna come and see us if they're scared of being murdered."

Mitsuhiro shrugged. The taxi rolled down the street, the meter clicking loudly every few seconds. "I can't say, sir. That's just what I heard."

No. It wasn't another host. I looked down at my shirt, hidden behind the bag.

"Say, you haven't seen a woman around here in a trench coat lately, have you? She was wearing a flu mask as well."

Mitsuhiro contemplated a moment and then shook his head. "I can't say I have, no. Why? Is she causing you trouble?"

"No, nothing like that. Just seems odd, don't you think?"

"What does, sir?"

"Why would a woman be wearing a trench coat in the middle of summer? Rakucho is already one of the hottest places around at the best of times, but in summer the heat can get unbearable, you know." It reminded me of my first summer there, after I ran away from home. I had no idea what I was in for or what I was going to do, but the sweat drenched through my clothes and the humidity was suffocating. I was from up north, a much colder area, and I honestly thought I was going to die. Of course, I was just a stupid kid, but it didn't change the fact that Rakucho was hot. All the buildings running late into the night, and all the bodies; Rakucho never slept and the heat never let up. Winter was the only real bearable time of year.

"I can't say I would know why, sir. Perhaps she feels more comfortable that way. Not everybody reacts to heat the same way, you know?"

"Yeah, maybe…"

We drove the rest of the way home in silence, and I gave Mitsuhiro a bow as he pulled back out into the street. "By the way, sir," he stopped to lean out the window, "your line of credit has been declined. This one's on the house, but you might want to look into it."

He waved and drove off. Why was everything getting declined? I cracked another drink, threw the empty bottle in the trash, and went upstairs. Maybe it was just my imagination, but the pounding in my head seemed to have decreased compared to the day before. Maybe those vitamin drinks were legit. I flicked the TV on for some noise as I went to the toilet, and the announcer's voice echoed throughout the room.

"Breaking news! Police have reported another dead body discovered in Rakucho just a short while ago…"

I stuck my head out the door to see the TV.

"Police have yet to confirm the man's identity, but they believe he worked in Rakucho. While they are hesitant to link this to yesterday's crime, in which another body was discovered outside a club called Serenity, they have refused to rule out that the incidents are not connected."

I flushed the toilet and ran back out, but the announcer had already moved on to the next news item. Another dead body? The blood on my shirt seemed to spread and the smell of iron assaulted my nostrils. I ripped the shirt off, popping several of the buttons, and threw it in the washing machine.

Her. It was her. The trench coat woman.

7

THE HOSTS OF CLUB TENSHI were in a panic. Even the boss was inside, trying to calm everyone down.

"Alright, alright, shut the hell up and listen!" He held his hands up and everyone fell silent. It was just before opening time and I noticed a few familiar faces were missing. Sadly, Haruki was still there. "As you all know, they found another body early this morning. I've been checking around and I've confirmed that he was one of Hot Love's boys."

The hosts broke out into an uproar again. The boss held his hand up and waited for everyone to stop talking.

"He's only been working here for a few months, just like the guy from Serenity. Now, as a precaution, I've told some of our newer hosts to stay home tonight." Whispers. "Just until we know what's going on." That explained the smaller numbers than usual. "The police may drop by to visit tonight." Groans. "I know, I'm not happy about it either, but we need to keep them happy or they'll find a reason to close us down. You all know how it works, so best behaviour tonight, boys."

"We're always on our best behaviour!" Haruki said over the crowd, then turned to look at me. "Well, most of us." I narrowed my eyes, but the boss ignored it.

"I don't care what you usually do or don't do. This is a special case. Best behaviour or you're fired. I'm not losing my club because you can't keep it in your pants, or you shoot your mouth off at some cop. If you have any grudges or misgivings, leave those at the door right now or get out. If the cops come in tonight to check things out, they are even more important than the women you're entertaining. Understand?" Murmurs. "I said, do you understand?"

"Yes, sir!"

A few moments later two of the newer hosts shuffled over towards the boss. After a few tense words they made their way up the stairs and didn't return. I stifled a laugh.

"I believe one of those kids comes from a less than savoury background." Koji's voice startled me.

"Geez, warn someone before you do that, huh? And who cares, we all come from different backgrounds and none of them are savoury. He's just chickening out."

Koji shook his head. "You ran away, it's not the same as someone who used to be in a gang. I believe he used to lead one of the numerous colour gangs that have been growing in number here recently."

I groaned. "Those punks? He was one of them?"

Koji nodded.

"They do realise that colour gangs went out of style when I was a kid, right? Nobody thinks that's cool anymore."

Koji shrugged. "Everything finds a way of coming back around again. Perhaps they're doing it ironically. Perhaps they look up to the old gangs. Who knows?"

I snorted. "Well, these little shits need better hobbies. Things are already tense enough around here without their help."

"On that note, I haven't seen your buddy around here for a while. What was his name, Yotchan?"

"Yotchan!" I laughed. Come to think of it, he hadn't been around for a while.

"I know the boss was trying to get him to join for a while. Said that his dashing good looks would make him one of the most successful hosts around. I think he's disappointed that he hasn't popped in for a while because he can't hassle him some more about it."

"Yotchan's busy with his... stuff... you know?" Yotchan was a mid-tier lieutenant for one of the local yakuza gangs, and one of the first friends I ever made in Rakucho. For a time it was uncertain which way either of us would go, but I ended up in the host business and he with some low-level gangs until the yakuza themselves picked him up. He could easily have outdone me as a host. He was tall, strikingly handsome, and well-built. But he wasn't a great conversationalist and spoke better with his fists than his mouth. As time went on, we saw each other less and less, although I still counted him as one of my closest friends.

"Maybe you should call him over for a bit. For, you know, protection." Koji's cheeks flushed red. I narrowed my eyes and then forced my lips together to stop from smiling.

"Koji, are you... do you...?"

"What?" I zipped my mouth shut, and he glared. "*What?*"

"I get it now. All this time I was so blind."

"You get what?"

I leaned forward. Koji leaned down to meet me. "You've got a crush on Yotchan?"

Koji slapped me on the shoulder and I laughed. A few of the hosts turned to look at us and I bit my lip. "I'm sorry, Koji, it's just too good. I honestly had no idea."

"You shut the hell up, Narumi."

"No, no, I get it, I really do. That is one handsome man." Another giggle escaped my lips. I coughed and stood up straight. My hip cracked and Koji's eyes were drawn to the sound. "What? Joints crack, you know."

"When you're old."

I slapped him over the side of the head and he smiled. Koji was a good friend. How had I missed his feelings for Yotchan all this time?

"I don't know if the boss would be so happy with him here and all the police around. But I'll let him know. I'm sure the boss would be happy to see him again soon anyway, someone else he can turn his attentions to."

"You know that he always gets what he wants." Koji agreed.

"Except Yotchan."

"Except Yotchan." The one who got away. Kinda. He was undoubtedly making more money with the yakuza than I was, but at least my work was legal.

"By the way, Koji."

"Hmm?"

"If you see a woman outside in a trench coat… Don't go near her, okay?"

"Why's that?"

I shook my head. "Just a feeling." The blood on my shirt was more than just a feeling, but I couldn't tell anyone about that. Not yet. "Oh yeah, and this might sound a little silly but… has everyone been getting paid as usual lately?"

Koji tilted his head. "Of course. Why?"

"Nothing." I woke up too late to call the bank. Where was all my money going then?

"Have you been spending too much again?" Koji's voice drew me back, and all of a sudden the music flared to life. It was close to opening time, and everything had to be perfect for the polices' arrival.

"What do you mean, again?"

"Narumi, you're awful with money."

"I am not!"

"When was the last time you invested in something?"

"The hell does that have to do with anything?"

"What was the last thing you bought?"

"…Vitamin drinks."

"That's not what I mean. Your last impulse buy."

"…I bought a new bed a few weeks ago."

Koji nodded. "And how old was your previous bed?"

I shrugged. "I dunno. A year or so."

"Uh huh. What did you do with it?"

"What is this, twenty questions? I called the removalists to take it away."

"Uh huh. And how long have you been in this current apartment?"

"What the hell does that matter?"

Koji leaned forward so I could hear him over the music. "It matters because you like the high life, Narumi. You need this job more than it needs you. That's why you don't want to leave. You spend money like it's water, and I'm sorry, but someone has to tell you. By the sounds of it, it's already too late."

His words slowly sank in. Another host filed past, lowering his head as he exited. Another quitter. Soon there would be barely enough hosts left to open for the night. Well, all the more for me. Koji might have been right on one thing. Maybe I did like to spend money. Maybe I was frivolous at times. But who wasn't? I didn't work so I could die and leave everything behind. I worked to enjoy my life. But he was wrong about me needing the job. I didn't need it. I would be perfectly fine without it. I enjoyed it, and the customers needed me, not the other way around. Otherwise, what, they'd be stuck with someone like Haruki? No-one deserved that.

"Doesn't look like he's going anywhere," I muttered, ignoring Koji's last statement. He lined up clean glasses and prepared a few buckets of champagne.

"Of course not. He is the number one host, after all."

"For now," I reminded him. Koji rolled his eyes.

"I'm not getting into your petty high school fights."

"It's not petty. He's an awful person."

"We're all awful people, aren't we?"

The question took me by surprise.

"What do you mean by that?"

He shrugged and shook his head. "Nothing. Anyway, it looks like several people have gone home, so I hope you're ready for a busy night."

"I'm always ready."

Haruki slapped the boss on the shoulder and laughed a little too loud at something he said. Part of me hoped that he would be the next victim found. Nobody deserved it more.

8

THE PHONE RANG THREE TIMES before he picked up.

"Yotchan!"

"Narumi?"

"Long time no see! How've you been?"

"Okay. You?"

Ever the conversationalist. I fingered the mask on my face. It was wet, sure, but how could I tell it was doing anything?

"Yeah, okay. I'm sure you can imagine how things have been over here the last few days." Silence. "The murders…"

"Ah."

I rolled my eyes. "I don't suppose you know anything about those, do you?"

"Not really. We heard about them, but uh, we've had other things on our plate recently. Things have been kinda busy." He sounded distant, like he had other places to be.

"You okay, Yotchan?"

"Yeah, sure. Just stuff."

"Sure… stuff. Look, that reminds me, I wanted to ask you something." Silence. Getting the man to talk was like pulling teeth. "I need a gun." Another brief silence.

"What do you need a gun for?"

"Because hosts are being murdered." He wasn't the sharpest tool in the shed, either.

"So, why do you need a gun?"

"Because I'm scared that I'll be next." Geez. The police ended up not getting around to Club Tenshi, nor did I see the trench coat woman on my way home, either. But she was there, constantly, on the fringes of my mind. She was lurking, waiting for her chance. She knew who I was; of course she did, my face was right there on the biggest sign in Rakucho, smack bang in the centre. If she was picking off hosts, it wouldn't be long until she turned to the big guns, and that meant me.

"I can't just get you a gun, Narumi."

"Why not?"

"I don't even have a gun."

"And you call yourself a yakuza?" I laughed, but he didn't.

"It's not that simple. There are a lot of laws now, and the punishments are much harsher than they used to be. If you're that scared, carry a knife like everyone else."

A knife? That wasn't going to do me much good. If she was close enough for me to stab, then she would also be close enough to stab me. I wanted her kept at a safe distance. At all times. I sighed.

"Fine. Look, how's things? The boss has been

50

talking about you. He hasn't seen you around for a while." It was a half-lie. The best type of lie. I pushed the mask into my cheek and the moisture bubbled. People really used these things?

"Yeah, fine. Been busy. That's all."

I sat down on the couch and felt the burgeoning fat around my midsection squish up over my jeans. Wonderful.

"Yotchan?"

"Yeah?"

"You go to the gym, right?"

"Yeah."

"Next time you go, can you take me?"

Yotchan laughed. For the first time in what felt like years, he laughed. What a foreign sound that had become. "You want to go to the gym?"

"What? What's so funny about that?"

"The gym doesn't serve alcohol, you know."

"Very funny, asshole. I… I lost my top spot this month." Silence. No, "I'm sorry, that must be very difficult for you" or even, "Oh, my condolences." Just silence. "People have been talking about my retirement. I don't want to retire. I still have years left in me, and besides, I enjoy my work." As I lit up a cigarette, I looked around my lavishly decorated apartment that I spent very little time in. Yes, it was true, I also enjoyed the money as well. All of that would dry up if I retired. I had my savings, sure… Or at least, I thought I did. Keeping track of money was never my strong point.

"Sure, whatever. But I hit the gym pretty early."

"What's early to you?"

"4 a.m."

"Ah, so after work! Great!"

"You can't come to the gym drunk, Narumi."

"I don't get drunk anymore!"

"No, because you're always drunk to begin with."

He wasn't much of a talker, but I missed Yotchan's casual banter. As young teens with too much time on our hands and no money, I was always the quick talker who got us out of trouble while Yotchan was the brawler who got us out of even bigger trouble. Why did we start drifting apart? Was is true, did people really drift apart for no good reason as they got older?

"I just need to lose some weight and build a little muscle. Yeah, I'm a bit older than these younger guys now so it takes a little more to keep up, but not like I've got one foot in the grave. I'm only 36." People were carrying on like I was in my 60s and ready to retire from the world. In most careers this was the age where everything fell into place.

"Uh huh. Look, 4 a.m. Be there or don't."

"You're a good man, Yotchan."

"I dunno about that."

I didn't know how to respond to that.

"Are you sure you're okay?"

"Yeah. Like I said, just work stuff."

"Okay. Well, I'll see you at the gym then."

"Yeah." He hung up. I looked at the phone a moment and then put it down. Something was up with him, but what?

I loosened the buckle on my belt and sighed. Maybe a walk before bed. The sun was rising anyway. It then hit me that it was awfully early for

Yotchan to be awake. I'd have to ask him about it at the gym.

I grabbed a knife from the kitchen drawer, threw the mask in the bin, and then locked the door behind me. Just in case. My skin did feel a little smoother.

9

A GANG OF PUNKS IN green clothing gathered around someone at the end of the road. They laughed as they pushed and shoved. A woman fell to the ground, clutching her bag and hiding her face at the same time.

"Hey! What do you little fucks think you're doing?"

I ran over to the woman and stood before her. These green punks were getting out of hand. Occasionally I saw groups of kids walking around in red, blue, and even purple, but overwhelmingly Rakucho was full of these green kids. They were like gnats, and every time you looked, there were more of them dirtying up the place.

"What's it to you?" one of them stepped forward. He was a great deal larger than the other boys, but something told me he was the brawn and not the brains.

"What's it to me?" I turned and indicated the

woman on the ground behind me. "Have you no respect?"

They laughed like it was the funniest thing they'd heard all day. "Respect? What's it to ya, grandpa?"

My cheeks flushed with rage. I took a step closer towards the boy and looked up at him, our noses almost touching. "Yeah, well in *grandpa's* day we knew not to mess with people older than us, and especially not to touch women."

Someone scrambled to their feet behind me and I realised the woman was running away. Good. She didn't need to be around for this any longer. If she had any wits about her, she'd report the incident to the police, but I feared they also had bigger things on their plate.

"Funny, because it ain't your time anymore." The boy pushed forward with his chest, trying to nudge me off balance. The punks behind him made no attempt to stifle their laughter. This was even better than picking on a defenceless woman, apparently. "So, why don't you go back to the nursing home you crawled out of and leave us to deal with the pretty women."

I stood my ground. Despite his size, this kid probably wasn't even born when I first started learning how to survive on the streets of Rakucho. She'd raised me, and I'd seen a lot worse than him in my time.

"How old are you?" I asked.

His brow furrowed, confused. "What's it to ya? You wanna date or something? I'm not into guys, you know."

His friends roared with laughter. Yes, he was clearly not the brains of the bunch.

"How long have you been here?" I changed the question.

"Been where?"

It was like talking to a brick.

"Here. Rakucho. When did you first come to Rakucho? Does that make it simpler? If I word it that way, does it get through the concrete barrier of your puny little mind?"

He grabbed the front of my shirt and lifted me. I gulped down my surprise. Okay, he was a little stronger than I thought. That changed nothing.

"Listen, you old fuck. We've wasted too much time playing with ya already. So it's time for you to fuck off and get out of our faces."

One of the punks behind him stepped forward. I recognised him from the other night.

"You," I spat.

He tilted his head. "Do I know you? Have we robbed you before or something?"

"We ran into each other the other night. You ran off with your tail between your legs, if I recall correctly."

He grinned. "Funny, doesn't ring a bell, and I've no idea who you are. My bad, gramps, but as much as I seem to have left an impression on you, you're nothing to me."

The gang laughed and slapped each other. This was all one big game of who had the biggest dick. I looked up at the sign next to us. "You do realise who you're talking to, right?"

The kid looked up at the sign and back at me.

His eyes flickered between us a few times and then he shrugged. "What? What am I supposed to be looking at?"

I pointed to the picture of myself, top and centre. "That's me, you numbnut."

He shook his head and shrugged. "That means nothing to me, gramps. All you pussies look the same. Besides, the guy in that photo looks at least ten years younger than you. You trying to get by on someone else's fame?" The boys snickered. "How lame."

"I've been making a living in Rakucho since before you were even born!" I didn't know why it was getting to me, but my blood boiled. How were they so disrespectful?

"Hey, if you really are a host—and looking at you, that's kinda debatable—then we're not the ones you should be worried about." Another boy stepped out of the pack and around the giant oaf. He motioned for the big boy to put me down. His hair was slicked back, and he adjusted his glasses. He wasn't the type I'd pick at first glance to join a colour gang, but apparently I knew nothing about kids these days.

"You mean the woman?"

The kid sized me up. "Although, you probably don't have too much to worry about. From what I hear, she likes them young and pretty."

Laughter. Yet my heart beat wildly in my chest.

"What do you know about her? Have you seen her?" It was her. This was proof. They knew about her! Of course they did, the colour gangs were all over Rakucho, and in larger numbers than us hosts.

If she was around, they would have seen her.

"What's it to you?"

I grabbed the kid by the lapels and yanked him hard. His buddies took a step forward to defend his honour, but he held a hand up. Didn't once lose his cool. So, this was the real leader.

"What's it to me? Someone is murdering hosts. If you know anything about her, you need to tell me right now."

He placed a steady arm on top of mine and pushed down, releasing my grip. He shrugged his shoulders back, smoothed his shirt, and cricked his neck. Just like Yotchan used to do back in the day, although physically Yotchan was closer to the oaf in size.

"If you wanna know, it'll cost you."

I scoffed, unable to hide my disbelief. "It'll cost me? Are you serious?"

He shrugged and turned to leave. "You're the one who wants to know. I'm not obligated to tell you anything."

I put a hand on his shoulder and he turned suddenly, his eyes flashing with anger. As fast as it appeared, it was gone.

"How much?"

A few boys giggled.

"How much you got?"

I pulled my wallet out and sighed. Inside was bare. I pulled the few notes that were in there out. "3,000 yen."

It was apparently the funniest thing they'd ever heard, but the leader pinched the notes and shoved them into his back pocket. "If that's all you make as a host, you're clearly not a very good one."

I clenched my jaw. "Just tell me what you know."

He shrugged. "A woman in a trench coat bumped into one of ours a few nights back." I nodded. Yes, yes, that was her. "He attempted to follow her and when he grabbed her arm, she pulled out a knife from beneath her coat. It was covered in blood. He didn't want no trouble, so he ran off. That's it."

"…That's it?"

"I told you we had info. Now you have it."

"I gave you 3,000 yen for that?" I fumed.

"Consider it a donation to a worthy cause. And if I were you, I'd get outta town for a while. She doesn't bother anyone else, but she seems to have a hard on for you guys. How much is your job worth? Your life?"

He raised his eyebrows and then jerked his head. His pack of greens moved out as he gave me one last look over. "But like I said, she seems to like them young, so you probably don't have much to worry about." He snickered and raised a hand in the air. "Later, gramps. And next time, don't interfere with our business, or that woman won't be the only thing you have to worry about!"

10

AFTER A CALL TO THE bank, they told me my credit card was maxed out. They had temporarily halted my line of credit and all I had to rely on was the money in my savings account. I popped the card in the ATM for the first time in what felt like years and cringed at the number staring back at me. I rubbed a hand over my cheek. My skin felt softer immediately after the mask, but now it was rough like normal. The lines that were etched into my face were as deep as ever, and my cheeks were most definitely not as smooth as a baby's bottom. I removed the card and sat in the gutter.

What was I going to do? How had I burnt through money so fast without realising it? My lifestyle wasn't that extravagant, was it? Koji's words came back to mind, but no. That wasn't it. He just didn't understand. All of those expenses were work expenses. I often brought customers home, and I couldn't bring them back to a hovel.

After hours dates were expensive, and the women spent good money on them. It was only good form to do the same in return.

And yet... where had all my money gone?

"She seems to like them young, so you probably don't have much to worry about."

The boy's words circled around my mind. The masks were a no-go, and murderous stalker or not... I needed money. I needed clients. Haruki was stealing my business, and all because he was younger than me. First impressions mattered. If a client spent five minutes with both of us, then it was no contest, but he was young and good looking, so they were moving over to him first. If I could get rid of that advantage, then they would all come back to me. I could fill my bank account again. I could continue the lifestyle I was so accustomed to.

I pulled out my phone and started typing. *Plastic surgery Rakucho.* A few seconds later some nearby clinics popped up. There were more than I expected. I straightened up a little. See. Everyone got a little work done here and there, nothing to be ashamed about. These clinics wouldn't exist unless they had business, and that many in one area meant business was booming. I smiled. For the first time in a while, I could see the light at the end of the tunnel. Problem solved!

A quick search through their websites soon brought my hopes crashing back to earth. They were expensive. Not just kind of expensive, but "I would need to sell my house and everything I owned just to get a foot in the door" expensive. Well, shit. I clicked on the link for a place called

CHAPTER TEN

"Smiling Bright," one of the last on the list.

Are you looking to turn your life around? At Smiling Bright, we can turn the clock back and return you to the smiling days of your youth. No more wrinkles, no more lines, no more age spots. No job too big or small. Reasonable prices and credit also available to approved cases. Not sure if we meet your needs? Call Smiling Bright for a free consultation right now!

A free consultation. At the very least I could do that. The reviews were heartening as well.

"Dr Nakata is a miracle worker! Within three simple visits he erased all my wrinkles! I feel like a 20-year-old again and my husband agrees!"

"I was unsure about whether plastic surgery was for me, but Dr Nakata was very forthcoming and open about everything that would take place. I was concerned about sagging skin, but now you can't even tell that I had a facelift!"

"I've hated my nose ever since I was a child. The kids always called me nasty names like 'troll' and 'ogre'. After visiting Dr Nakata, now I'm beating the men off with sticks!"

It was almost *too* good to be true. But, it was free consultation, and they were open until late. I could get in before work. I dialled the number.

"Smiling Bright, how may I help you?"

I stood up and slinked around the corner, away from the crowds. "Hi, um, I was wondering if I could book a consultation?"

"Of course, sir. When would you like to come in?"

"When's the earliest slot you have available?"

The sooner the better.

"We have a slot free tomorrow at 4 p.m., sir."

"Tomorrow? Excellent! And, it's free, right?"

"Yes, sir. All consultations are free." Her voice was pleasant and reassuring. I smiled.

"Good, good. And… confidential, I assume?"

"Of course, sir. Our customers' privacy is of the utmost importance. We even have a back entrance should you wish to remain unseen."

Oh, they were good.

"Excellent, excellent. That sounds wonderful. Okay, 4 p.m. tomorrow then."

"Of course. Could I have your name, sir?" My name. Shit. Of course. She must have heard my hesitation. "It's just so we know who to call out for, sir. It doesn't have to be your real name. The doctor will deal with all of that in private."

I laughed. "Haha, of course. Um, Narumi." I slapped myself in the head the moment I said it.

"Narumi. Of course, sir. We'll see you tomorrow."

"Yeah, sure, tomorrow." I hung up. Idiot. Oh well, it didn't matter that much. It was just a consultation, nothing else. Maybe the doctor knew of a way to help smooth out some of the lines on my face and make my skin shine again. That was all I needed. A chance to compete with the younger boys visually again. I could do everything else after that.

Everything was going to turn out just fine. I smiled.

11

A YOUNG WOMAN IN A face mask stepped through
the doorway to Club Tenshi and my heart caught in
my throat. *Her.* It was her. It had to be. Unable to
tear my eyes off her as she stood there, looking
around the club, I banged on the bar a few times to
get Koji's attention over the music. He ran over to
the door and smiled at the woman, then bowed
deeply.

"Ah, ma'am, nice to see you here again."

My feet seemed to carry me to the door of their
own accord.

"Hi," I said, my voice breaking. She dipped her
head slightly and then continued to look over my
shoulder. There was no trench coat, but she was
wearing a mask. Suspicious.

"Here to see Haruki again?" Koji said. She
nodded silently. "Right this way, ma'am." Koji led
the woman past me, giving me an angry glance as
he did so. I took a step back and out of their way

long after they'd already passed.

"What is wrong with you?" Koji returned as the woman sat down with Haruki. He kissed her on the cheek and made a loud show about something and another of the younger hosts sat down with them.

"That's her," I said. "That's the woman."

"Who? What woman?"

"The trench coat woman! That's her! You let her in!"

Koji looked over at the woman and then back at me a few times. He was thoroughly perplexed. "Are you high?"

"It's her!" I repeated. "The mask! She wears a mask!" I fumbled for the phone in my pocket and Koji snatched it from me.

"Narumi."

"What?"

"You don't remember her?"

I stopped. Haruki and the host on the other side of the woman clinked glasses. She held hers close to her knees, but she didn't drink.

"Should I?"

Koji shook his head. "How you ever became the top host, let alone kept the position, I'll never know."

My brows furrowed in anger. "And just what is that supposed to mean?"

Koji slammed the phone back in my hands and returned behind the bar.

"Honestly… You really don't recognise her?"

I sat down at the bar again and lit a cigarette. "No…"

"Well, you should. She used to be one of your

regulars."

I watched the woman as Haruki and his friend... what was his name... Jotaro? Junta? Junpei? Something like that. The little buff bald dude that looked like he had no business being a host. Was Haruki bringing him into his circle? They laughed and cheered and lavished attention on the woman, refilling their empty glasses and offered her some more. She refused, so they downed their own again and continued carrying on like they were having the time of their lives. Considering how much money she was spending without actually drinking herself, they probably were.

"I don't remember her."

Koji placed a beer in front of me. "Do you ever wonder why Haruki claimed your spot?"

My brows knitted in confusion and anger. "Because he's young and good looking."

Koji tsked a few times. "That doesn't hurt, no, but it's because he remembers details, Narumi. He remembers their names. He remembers who he's seen before and he remembers who he's seen with other hosts as well."

I swallowed half the beer at once. "What are you saying?"

Koji leaned forward over the bar. "I'm saying that he paid more attention to your clients than you did and now they're his clients. You get it?"

"...He stole my customers?"

Koji dried a glass and raised his eyebrows in return. "You're a genius."

I stood up. "He stole my customers?!" The words came out louder than I intended and everyone turned our way… The woman included. Koji pushed me back down in the chair.

"How many customers did you entertain last night?"

"I don't know, what does it matter?"

"You entertained five women last night, Narumi. Five. Do you remember any of their names?"

"Sure, there was… Mikiko, and…" My voice trailed off. Koji was already frowning at me. "Okay, so I don't remember their names. That's not important! Making them feel special is!"

Koji laughed and shook his head. "I don't know how you survived this long, I honestly don't."

I finished the beer and looked back at the woman. She never took her mask off, but she smiled and nodded at all the right points and let Haruki and his little bald friend do all the talking. She did look familiar, I had to admit, but I couldn't recall who she was. Her eyes flickered over to me every now and then, and then looked away when she realised I was watching.

"How long has she been seeing Haruki?" I asked.

"Not long. A week or two now."

"Did she always have the mask?"

"No, just the last few weeks. I think she got some work done, and she's waiting for the swelling to go down. She doesn't drink, but she pays for everyone else to."

Odd.

"She was very into you, you know."

"What?" They weren't words I was expecting to hear. Koji leaned forward again so I could hear him better over the music.

"If I'm honest, she was always a little plain. I think that's why she got the work done. I don't know what she does in the outside world, but she's clearly very well paid and has never held back in here. Maybe she decided it was finally time to get some work done, I don't know. But she always looked at you with the most lovey-dovey eyes. I'm surprised you never noticed."

I was also surprised. At a lot of things. Then it hit me. That was why I didn't recognise her. Deep in the recesses of my brain sat a woman, incredibly average in every way. She was the same height and build as the woman sitting with Haruki, although her hair was tied in a simple ponytail, not like it was now; out and slightly permed. I couldn't remember her name, but I had memories of her spending a lot of money when she came to see me. I never took her home with me, but we did go on an after-hours date a few times. She was pleasant enough, but not my type.

"Huh."

"Now you remember?"

I nodded. "If she was so fond of me, like you say, then why is she with Haruki?"

"Seriously?"

"What?"

"You're an idiot."

I held my glass in front of him and indicated he pour another beer. Several coughs racked my body, and I washed them back down with the cold alcohol.

"So, what you're telling me is that I need to remember their names and they'll come back to me?"

Koji slapped me upside the head again. "No, you barbarian. But maybe you need to start thinking about who you're even talking to. Haruki may be a fake, but he's real good at making women think otherwise."

"What's her name?"

"Seriously?"

"Just tell me her name, Koji."

"Mizuki."

"Right." I gulped down the rest of the beer, slammed the glass down, and walked over to Haruki. Koji called out behind me but I ignored him. Mizuki.

"Hi!" I painted my best smile on as I sat down. Joichi? Joichiro? quickly disappeared. Haruki faked his best smile to greet me.

"Narumi! I see you're free yet again. What brings you to see us?"

"Mizuki." I turned my attentions to the woman in the mask. "It's been a while!" I did my best to hide a smile as Haruki's face dropped. The woman nodded a few times, unable to meet my eyes.

"Ah, yes, hello. Nice to see you again."

"How is Haruki treating you? He's been *very* busy recently, so many women, all day and night, it's truly amazing how he has time for them all."

"Some of us are just young enough to keep up, I guess," he said through gritted teeth. I placed my arm on the chair behind the woman.

"How have you been, Mizuki? I haven't seen you in a while." She seemed to flinch and continued to stare at the floor.

"I've... been busy..."

"So I hear. I was thinking that I hadn't seen you in a while. I missed you, you know."

Even through her mask I could see the blush rising on her cheeks. Checkmate.

"Anyway, if you don't mind, we're in the middle of—"

"Oh, of course, sorry. I just saw Mizuki here and thought I'd say hello. It's been so long and she's always been one of my favourite people to see. You better treat her right, or you'll be answering to me!"

I grabbed Mizuki's hand, kissed it, and then made my exit. Koji coughed and hid his face as I sauntered back over to the bar and sat down.

"You're shameless."

"Women like details. They like to feel important." I took the beer he placed in front of me and smiled. "Let Haruki sit with that for a while."

Fifteen minutes later the woman—Mizuki— stood up and made her way back to the door. She looked up at me briefly as she passed by and then nodded and cast her eyes back to the ground. Her shyness was almost endearing. I smiled back.

"Hope to see you back here again soon, Mizuki. It's not the same without you!" A bit much, perhaps, but she smiled and made her way up the stairs as Koji held his hand out for her to follow. I moved over to the doorway and put a hand on his shoulder. "See. Easy."

As she reached the top of the stairs, my stomach dropped. She grabbed a brown trench coat, put it on slowly and deliberately, and then looked down right at me. Her eyes smiled before she disappeared back

into the darkness that was Rakucho.
It was her.

12

A TALL, BROAD MAN GRUNTED as he squatted. Even at a distance I knew it was Yotchan; there was no mistaking that size.

"Yo, Yotchan!" I called out across the empty gym. Aside from Yotchan, only three people were working out. Even for a big city gym, it seemed people didn't want to get up early. He ignored me and continued grunting. Sweat dripped from his forehead and he racked the bar with a loud bang.

"You actually came."

"Nice to see you, too."

He grabbed a towel and wiped his face. He wore a dark tracksuit despite the disgusting heat outside, drenched from head to toe in his own sweat.

"Isn't that hot?"

"It's the only way they'll let me in," he said.

"Ah…" His tattoos. "So, they know?"

He nodded. "I don't make a fuss, they don't make a fuss. Anyway, we're not here to train your mouth, come on."

My workout clothes consisted of some old shorts I'd dug out the bottom of my drawers and an equally old singlet. I had no doubt my skin was glowing from how little sunlight it had seen.

"You're right, you are looking a little soft," Yotchan said, slapping my stomach with the back of his hand.

"Thanks, you know all the right things to say."

"I'm not here to be your mama."

"No, you were never very good at that, were you?"

Sharp-tongued as always, Yotchan removed some weights from the bar and motioned for me to step under it.

"Uh... What am I supposed to do?"

"Lift it."

"...I get that. But more specifically, what am I supposed to do?"

Yotchan wiped his face again and crossed his arms. "You put the bar on your back. You sit down. You stand up again. Repeat several times. Finish."

"...You're a terrible trainer, you know?"

"I'm not your trainer, and you're the one who wanted to come here. I'm quite happy on my own."

I looked at him a few moments before trying to put the bar on my back. There was nothing on it, but it felt strange, regardless. Something about the tone in Yotchan's voice and the dark look in his eyes worried me. I lifted the bar off and took a step back.

"Hey, this isn't so bad."

"Sit," Yotchan said. I sat like I was going to the toilet. "Stand." I stood back up. "Now do that a few more times."

"That's it?"

"That's it."

If it was this easy, why didn't everyone do it? Sneaky Yotchan, keeping all the fun to himself.

"Hey, Yotchan?" I asked while I squatted again.

"What?"

"What's going on?"

"What do you mean?"

I pushed back up. "You seem kinda down."

"Are you my wife now?"

"No, but I'd like to think I'm your mate." He said nothing. "I don't wanna pry or anything, but even for you, you seem kinda sullen."

"I'm a sullen guy."

I put the bar back on the rack and shook my arms out. I grinned. "Easy!"

"Good. Now let's put weights on it."

My face dropped as he loaded several heavy plates onto the formerly empty bar.

"Aren't you gonna—"

"I'd rather watch you fall flat on your face first."

"Thanks…"

I got back under the bar, Yotchan grinning out the corner of my eye as he watched. Well, at least he was smiling. I lifted the bar with a great heave and took a shaky step back. "This won't kill me, right?"

"Probably not."

"Probably… Wonderful. Well, if you're not gonna talk, I will. I need your help."

I sat down and my thighs screamed in pain. I let out a surprised grunt and pushed back up on wobbly legs. Yotchan snickered.

"If you've got time to talk, then I need to put more weight on."

"No!" I grunted. "Just... a minute..." I sat down again and pushed back up, nearly falling forward on my face as I did so. I quickly put the bar back in its place and wobbled back. "Okay. Yes. Well. That's quite enough of that."

Again Yotchan laughed through his nose and loaded several more plates back onto the bar. I stepped out of the rack and watched him smoothly get under the bar, step back, and squat the weight like it was nothing.

"You know about the recent murders in Rakucho, right?" I decided to broach the subject right away.

"I do." He grunted, beads of sweat forming around his temple.

"I think I know who it is."

"And?"

"And...?" And what? She knew who I was, too. She was playing with me. The first host was to get my attention. The second she killed deliberately when she knew I was nearby. She bumped into me on purpose. Then she had the audacity to come to my place of work and flaunt it in front of me. No-one would believe me; there was no proof and I would be called an imaginative drunk, or worse. She was coming after me, but she wanted to make sure I was thoroughly frightened first. It was working.

Yotchan racked his weights and wiped his brow. "What do you want me to do about it?"

I opened my mouth a few times before shrugging. "You can't... do something about her?"

He laughed out loud. The few people in the gym all turned to look at us at once. "What, you want me to whack her?" I held my hands up to shoosh him.

"Shh, not so loud! No, wow, let's not go from 0 to 100 quite that quickly."

He took a drink from his bottle. "Then what?"

"I... I don't know. But I'm scared, Yotchan. You hear me? I'm scared."

Yotchan put his bottle of water down, threw his towel over his shoulder, and stepped out of the rack. His movements were slow, calm, and measured, but the shaking of his fists otherwise betrayed his emotions.

"You're scared? Let me tell you something, Natchan." That was a name I hadn't heard in a while. Yotchan used to call me that when we were kids, but as we got older, it sounded more like a childish nickname so I asked him to stop. He never asked that I stopped calling him Yotchan, so I never did. Hell, I don't think anyone actually knew his real first name other than myself. Perhaps that was the way he liked it.

"Three days ago we got a call. One of the guys had been found dead in his apartment. The boss was ready to go to war. It took everything I had to stop him. He doesn't listen to me much these days, you see." His jaw clenched tight, and I unconsciously took a step back. "The thing is, no-one knows how he died. His door was locked and there were no signs of forced entry. He was just dead. No visible wounds, no blood, no signs of struggle, nothing."

"W-What happened?"

"What happened?" Yotchan laughed. He stood up to full height and scratched the back of his head. He looked up at the roof for a few more moments and then back at me. There were tears in his eyes. "I fucked up."

I tilted my head. "I don't... What do you mean?"

He sat on a nearby bench and covered his face with his hands. A few seconds later he looked back at me. "I fucked up, Natchan. I fucked up real good this time and there's nothing we can do."

I didn't know what to say, but he kept going.

"The next day we found one of our lieutenants floating in the river. Same again. No visible wounds, nothing. It was like he just dropped dead. The boss was livid. He wanted heads. Any heads. He was ready to go to war with anyone and everyone just to find out who was doing it. But that's the thing, Natchan."

"W-What's the thing?" He was scaring me. I'd never seen him like that before.

"It's not a person, Natchan. It's not..." He trailed off and stood up. "Look, I understand you're having some troubles right now, and I wish I could help, I really do." It was the most I'd heard Yotchan speak in years. I didn't know it was in him. He grabbed me by the shoulders and squeezed so tight I let out an involuntary gasp. "You've been a good friend, Natchan."

He kept saying my name. It frightened me even more.

"What are you—"

"Go to the police. If you really believe this

woman is after you, see the cops. There's nothing I can do for you. I don't think I'll be… Never mind. Maybe you should stay home for a few days, or take a holiday or something."

"I can't…" My bank account violently disagreed with that idea, as did my pride. Each night, fewer and fewer hosts were showing up to work; not just at Club Tenshi, but all around Rakucho. The customers needed entertaining. There was no better time than now to claw my way back to the top again. Coughs racked my body, nearly doubling me over with their intensity.

"And you should quit smoking while you're at it. That shit's gonna kill you."

"Not if she does first." I stood back up. There was an awkward silence, as though it was the last time either of us would see each other. Yotchan's life was a mystery to me. We could go months without talking to each other, and even longer without seeing each other. We lived and worked in the same area, but life took us in different directions and we were both busy adults now.

"Hey, Yotchan. Come stop by the bar tomorrow. For old time's sake."

"I can't. I have… things to do."

"Koji misses you."

He raised his eyebrows a moment and almost broke into a smile. Almost. "You mean he misses my money."

"Yeah, probably that too. And I miss you. Come for a drink. Just one. The boss won't shut up about you either."

"He also just wants my money." Silence. "We'll

see."

That was probably the best answer I was going to get out of him. I let the topic drop. Yotchan's eyes were bloodshot, and not from the uncharacteristic tears from earlier.

"When was the last time you slept?"

"I don't."

"What?"

"Sleep."

"Oh."

"You wanna finish this workout or not?" Before my eyes he reverted to the cold Yotchan of old. Talk time was over. He'd shared too much and now it was time to pretend that it had never happened.

"Sure," I said. "But only if you take some of those weights off. My knees are killing me."

13

LIGHTS TWINKLED IN THE DARKNESS above me. *SMILING BRIGHT* lit the night sky in huge letters. It didn't seem very private, but then again, everything in the neighbourhood was covered in gaudy signs and bright colours, so perhaps that was their way of blending in. A small sign beside the front entrance pointed to the back with an arrow. I followed it.

"Hi," I announced myself as I stepped inside. A short, dim corridor led to reception. A single person, an older woman, sat reading a magazine in the waiting area. I turned to the receptionist. "I, uh, have an appointment today."

The woman looked up from her computer and smiled. My heart did a mini-flip. She was gorgeous. I smiled back and ran a hand through my hair.

"Your name, sir?"

"N-Narumi." My heart pounded like a teenager. She didn't know it was my real name. No need to stumble over my words. I grinned through how stupid I felt.

"Of course, sir. If you'd like to sit down, the doctor will be with you in a moment."

I nodded, took one more glance, and then sat as far as I could from the other woman. I wore a cap and face mask, but I still felt naked and exposed. I had to get to work in a few hours, so things were going to be tight, but considering that few hosts were showing up in the first place, I still had the advantage.

The old woman didn't even look up from her magazine. I picked one up from the table in front of me and flicked through it. A fashion magazine from last month. I was good on that front. I picked up another. Huh. So the plastic surgery industry had their own magazine as well? I had been interviewed numerous times over the years for the *Host Monthly* magazine, which technically could be read by anyone, but was meant for working hosts all over the country. This seemed to be their version of it. The main article was an interview with a Dr Nakata, the head surgeon.

You've been working on numerous experimental procedures over the years, haven't you Dr Nakata? Could you tell us about those?

Well, I can't say too much about it because we're still in the testing stages and getting everything approved, but my latest procedure can make anyone look at least 10 to 20 years younger, regardless of the lifestyle you've led. Not only that, but we've made huge advancements in facial reconstruction, so we've had a lot of interest from the private sector from patients looking to fix scars from childhood accidents, disfigurements from accidents, and all other sorts of trauma. Our team is top notch, and our goal is to make everyone feel as beautiful on the outside as they are on the inside.

It sounded too good to be true. A voice calling my name drew my attention, and I quickly threw the magazine back on the table. "Yes! That's me!" The old woman looked over the edge of her glasses at me and then back at her magazine. "Sorry, yes."

A doctor stood beside the reception desk. He grinned. "Right this way."

I followed him down a separate corridor and he held a door open at the end for me. White fluorescent lights lit the room almost painfully. Numerous posters and awards covered the walls, and medical papers, journals, and folders lined several bookshelves. A single bed lay in the middle of a wide open space to the right of his desk, alongside a stack of medical tools in the corner. The room smelt clean. Hospital clean.

"Narumi?" The doctor held his hand out and I shook it. "I'm Dr Nakata. What brings you to see us today?"

I sat down in the chair before his desk with a small nod, removing my cap and mask.

"I, uh, I work as a host—"

"I see."

"—and, well, I guess, you know, it's been a rough few years. Lots of drinking and such." I couldn't stop the nervous laugh from escaping my lips. It was like trying to tell a parent about the vase you broke while they were out. "I just... well, if I could look a little younger again..."

Dr Nakata grinned. "Of course. That's what we do here after all. And there's no need to be nervous. We see young hosts here all the time."

"Really?" I perked up. That surprised me.

"Of course. While the outside world might see it as wasteful and narcissistic, we at Smiling Bright are all too aware of the demands of jobs such as yours, and the importance of looking your best."

I sighed with relief. This guy got it!

"So, what can you do for me?"

"Well, our simplest procedure can help to reduce wrinkles and lines from the problem areas. Particularly around the eyes, brow, and mouth." He grinned. "It doesn't even require surgery."

"Good, because that brings me to my next question. Um, how much does it cost?"

His grin grew larger. I gulped.

"If money is a concern, we do offer some more... experimental... procedures that we can fit to your budget."

"...Experimental?" Alarm bells went off in my brain. Get out of there. Get out of there fast. Already I could see him leaping over the desk, tying me down to the bed as a nurse ran in to restrain me while they cut out my organs or rearranged my face.

"Yes." The doctor stood up, grabbed a file from the shelf and placed it in front of me. He flicked through the pages. "We're currently going through the trial process of several procedures. All are fully backed by the medical authorities and closely monitored for any side effects or unexpected results. Because these procedures have not yet been fully approved for the public at large, we're able to offer our customers drastic reductions in price. In some cases, depending on the procedure and the customer, we can even offer these for free."

I swallowed again. The pictures showed various chemical mixes, diagrams of faces, and how the creams were to be applied. One page showed several incisions on a face, indicating the best places to cut and pull to eliminate wrinkles. I cringed, and the doctor noticed.

"All of these procedures are perfectly fine, I can assure you. We've already completed them successfully on numerous patients, all with stunning results. We need to reach a certain threshold before the authorities can approve them for general usage, but we've yet to have a single problem yet."

His words were convincing, and his silky smooth voice helped with his persuasive powers. Bigger than all of that though was the price. Free; or if not free, cheap enough that even I could afford it. Perhaps this was what I needed to get me back on my feet. He said that he treated several other hosts, and these were guys even younger than me! If they were having trouble keeping their youth, then I had nothing to be ashamed of!

"All you need to do is sign these waiver forms." The doctor removed another file from the cabinet behind me and placed it on the desk. They were less forms and more a booklet of terms and conditions. There was no way I could read through all of that right then and there, let alone hope to understand any of it. How did I know that somewhere in the tiny print I wasn't signing my life away to them?

"Can I have some time to look over all of this?"

"Of course." The doctor's grin reminded me of a hyena I'd seen on TV once, before it devoured the remains of a carcass. It grated with the silky tone of his voice. He sat down and clenched his hands together over his crossed legs. "Let me ask you something, Narumi. How old do you think I am?"

I was taken aback by the question. "Uh, I don't know. 35?" He did look young, but if he was an experienced doctor then he had to be older, so I lowballed the figure.

"I'm 58."

If I had been drinking, I would have spat it in his face. Instead, my eyes turned into saucers and I struggled to find words. "A-Are you for real?"

His grin grew almost lecherous. "I never attempt any procedure that I'm not happy to try on myself first. How can I proclaim the benefits of something unless I know them first hand?"

He honestly didn't look older than his mid-thirties. 58? He could easily be my father, and yet he looked like a colleague!

"That's amazing…"

"You'll be in good hands here, Narumi. We've taken care of many young men just like you. This is, however, and important decision, so I won't rush you. Feel free to take the forms home and read over them. You can let us know once you've made your decision, and then we can get to work right away. But, the clock is ticking. We only have so many slots left, and once they are gone, they're gone."

I fought the urge to answer with a resounding "yes" right then and there. That was one of my biggest failings, was it not? My inability to think something through before charging ahead with it. That's what people told me, anyway. Well, this level-headed adult was going to take some time to consider things carefully first.

"Thank you, Dr Nakata. I just need a little time to look all this over, if that's okay."

"Of course. And might I add, you have such lovely cheekbones." His eyes ran over my face like a scanner preparing to copy and print. "Magnificent, really. I think we can do some great work here. Easily double your income. Triple it, even!"

In the back of my mind, I wondered if Haruki was one of the hosts he had seen. His sudden rise to the top when he was as interesting as a rusty plank grated on me. If the doctor could really do what he promised, then...

"Thank you, doctor. I really appreciate you taking the time to see me today. I will definitely get back to you soon."

"Not at all. We await your call."

So did I. But first, work awaited.

14

I WAS DOWN TWO CANS of beer by the time I reached work, and three glasses at the bar when the boss came down. Drinking was one of the few times my mind cleared, perhaps from all the years of practice. Yotchan, the doctor, the trench coat woman, my bank account... Sweet ale brought peace, quiet, and a moment of respite. That was all I needed. Just a moment.

"Alright, gather around!" The boss stood in the middle of the club floor and the five hosts who had bothered to show up rushed over to him. He was not a man you wanted to keep waiting. Koji prodded my arm.

"What?"

"That means you too."

I rolled my eyes, finished the glass, and then staggered over. Haruki, unfortunately, was also still at work, either too stupid or unwilling to give up his newfound fame.

"We need to talk sales."

"Yay…" Everyone turned to look at me. "What?"

"Narumi, I suggest you shut your mouth," the boss said. "You especially ain't gonna like what's coming." Haruki snickered. All it would take was reaching out across the small space separating us and grabbing his neck to choke the life out of him. How satisfying that would be. Why hadn't the woman… what was her name again… Mizuno? Misako?… taken him yet? It *was* her, right? It had to be.

"Sales have fallen nearly 50% since all this started going down," the boss began. Nobody said a word, so he continued. "If this continues, we're going to have to close the bar."

"You can't do that!" I protested. He held a single finger up before me. The words died on my lips.

"I don't like this any more than you do, but it's not like we have much choice. People are scared, and as you can tell—" he held his hands out around him "—we're not exactly packed to the rafters. Which means that if we're going to avoid closing down, you guys are going to need to work harder to get people in here. We can't just rely on advertising and word of mouth anymore. Nobody wants to be somebody's last client, nor do they want to get attacked themselves just for being in the area."

"So you want us to go out and cold call people?" The disgust on Haruki's face was palpable. Poor baby didn't want to get his hands dirty doing commoner's work. What a piece of shit. That was how we found all our clients when I first started. I grinned.

"Yes, do you have a problem with that?" the boss replied. Haruki shook his head. "Good. Then shut up. Also, to give you shitheads the boost you need, I figured I'd tell you how the rankings stand for this month right now. These figures are just for the last two weeks, but if you want to see some changes, well, better start bringing some people in."

My heart jumped. Rankings? They only just changed the rankings on the board not that long ago. How much could have changed since then?

"Haruki is still our number one seller. Congratulations." Of course he was. Haruki beamed and a few of the other guys slapped him on the back. He looked at me and held his hands out as if to shrug. "Sucks to suck."

"Jo is in second. Well done, Jo. Just a few months ago you were barely making any sales. I dunno what changed, but keep at it!"

My heart sank. Jo? That... that bald kid that had been hanging out with Haruki lately? He'd only been with us for something like half a year! He wasn't exactly what you'd call a typical host either. He was clean shaven, short, and slightly more muscular than the average slim and tall host. He was like a buff monk. How the hell was he second?

"Narumi. You're in third." The boss stopped to look pointedly at me. "Sales are tanking hard."

I swallowed. The other guys were snickering, but the dots swimming around my vision blocked them out. Third? Tanking sales? I nodded, unable to form words.

Third.

I was third.

I was dropping even further, and it had only been a few weeks.

The boss finished his spiel and I returned to the bar. Koji handed me a fresh drink and Haruki sat down beside me.

"Retirement is always an option, old man."

Koji shook his head. He saw the look in my eyes.

"I suggest you get out of my personal space," I growled.

"Or what?"

I grabbed the front of his silk shirt and yanked him closer. "You know what."

He laughed. He wasn't even scared. He brushed my hand off and fixed his shirt. Running his fingers through his hair, he glanced at Koji and then walked away. "Shouldn't you be outside trying to find some housewives to entertain?" he said with his back turned. "Not that they pay much, but I'm sure it's better than nothing. No doubt they'd take pity on you."

"Leave him be," Koji said. I downed the beer and slammed the glass back on the bar.

"I'm gonna kill him."

"No you're not."

"I am. I'm going to grind his face into a pulp and then rip his insides out and feed them to the crows."

"He's just a kid acting tough. Leave him be. You were just like him once."

"I was never that bad."

"No, you were worse."

I stumbled as I pushed myself up from the bar. Koji's brow furrowed. "When did you start drinking?"

"Which time?"

"Maybe you should sit down for a bit. Someone needs to stay here anyway for the walk-ins."

"Are you trying to say that I can't bring any customers in?"

"That's not what I said, Narumi."

My face flushed with heat and my vision swam. Anger boiled within me and I wanted to take it out on anyone, it didn't matter who. Just get it out, because it was eating me up the longer I kept it in.

"But that's what you meant!"

"Look, why don't you go sleep it off for a bit out back. We've got things covered here."

"Why, so those little pissants can take even more of my money?"

"Narumi…"

"No. I am not washed up! You'll see!" I stumbled towards the door, grabbed the frame, and turned back to Koji. "You ain't seen nothing yet!"

I stumbled out into the street. Humid air poured over me like a wave, clinging to my skin like a wet curtain. Rotting trash stank up the area and remarkably fewer people than usual patrolled the night streets.

"Hey!" I attempted my best smile at two passing women. "Wanna grab a few drinks?" They screwed up their faces and hurried away. "Yeah, well, I didn't want to drink with you, anyway! You don't look like you could afford it!" I kicked a trash bag in my way and stumbled further down the street. Customers. Women to drink with. Money. Fame. Number one.

This was all their fault. I hadn't done anything wrong. Those little upstarts. Jo and Haruki. What did they know about entertaining women? About the business behind being a host? Nothing. They knew absolutely nothing. I'd show them. Tanking sales, my ass. I'd bring in more women than even I could handle. Spares, even, for those ungrateful assholes to show them how good I was. They'd see. They'd all see.

My head pounded, and the sky spread out above me. I didn't know how I got there, but next thing I knew I was lying in the gutter, my head throbbing like it was about to shatter. A woman stood above me.

"Hey. You wanna drink?" The words sounded foreign to my ears. My tongue wasn't able to form them properly. I rubbed my eyes a few times and blinked. My hands were sticky…

Blood?

My heart froze.

A trench coat billowed in the wind before me.

It was her. She'd finally come for me.

15

MY HANDS FELL TO MY chest, then my face, my arms, and my legs. I patted everywhere, looking for the source of the blood. Then I realised it wasn't me. It wasn't my blood.

The woman looked down at me. The bright lights of Rakucho shone behind her, casting an ominous silhouette as her hand dropped to her side. She was holding a rather large knife, blood dripping from it to the ground.

"W-Who are you?!" I tried to scream, but it came out as more of a croaked whisper. My throat was parched. How long had I been lying there? What happened? A few moments earlier I'd been walking the streets of Rakucho, and then... The woman looked at me for a few more moments in silence, and then turned her gaze to something beside me.

I screamed. I shuffled back on all fours until my back hit a tree and I pushed myself to my feet.

A body. Another dead body. By the looks of him, yet another host. I stepped forward and then turned to puke.

Jo. It was Jo.

"W-Why..." My throat burned and my head pounded like someone playing the drums on either side of my temples. The woman wiped the blood on the inside of her trench coat and then hid the knife in a pocket. My eyes flickered back and forth between her and the dead man I had been lying next to. Jo. Another host. The very same host that had just overtaken me in the preliminary rankings. The woman was calm and collected and made no movement towards me. As I took in our surroundings, I came to recognise where we were; the outskirts of Rakucho. My watch said 3 a.m. I'd been passed out for several hours. We were alone, but it wouldn't be long until somebody stumbled past on their way home and saw the dead body lying in the street, and the man covered in blood standing above him.

Then it hit me again. This wasn't the first time we'd had a run in after she'd murdered someone. Was she... framing me? A washed up host trying to regain his former glory days by picking off his younger rivals? I mean, it made sense. The police wouldn't have to dig hard to come up with that motive—he'd just overtaken me in sales—and once they had that, and the evidence of his blood all over me, well, they wouldn't need a weapon. That would be case closed. And that many bodies would mean the death penalty, first offence or not.

"Why are you doing this?" Again my scream

was more of a dying frog's croak. I cleared my throat and grabbed my head as it swam.

"You really don't remember?" Her voice was oddly deep. Or perhaps that was just in my head as my brain struggled to process everything.

"Remember what? Who are you?" I wiped my bloody hands on my shirt, but there was too much and it was beginning to dry. The woman stepped over Jo's body, but as she did, he gurgled. Her eyes widened, and she turned back to him.

He was still alive!

"Jo!"

She pulled out her knife with inhuman speed and plunged it into his chest. Over and over she struck him with furious speed, and then, as his final gurgles began to peter out, she placed the knife under his neck. Her eyes focused on mine, she pressed the knife in just under his ear and pulled it, slicing his neck from ear to ear. The gurgling stopped. She moved, standing over the man, and then straddled him. She placed the knife between his teeth and again turned to look at me. I closed my eyes and flinched as the sound of the knife tearing through his cheeks assaulted me.

My mouth refused to form words. My brain ran a mile a minute, forming questions faster than I could consciously recognise them. They refused or were unable to work in tandem, so instead I gaped at her like a dying fish on a dock.

She walked towards me, blood dripping from the knife to the ground below. Each drop resounded like a gunshot. Where was everyone? This was Rakucho, there ought to be someone around.

Anyone! I tried to scream for help, but only groaned.

The woman stood before me, close enough to reach out and grab. Close enough for her to plunge the knife into my heart and then mutilate me like she had Jo. Tiny, buff, un-host-like Jo, his jaw now lolling, barely hanging on to the rest of his face. Had she done that to her previous victims as well? Why hadn't the news reported on it? That seemed like a significant detail.

I steeled myself and tried to focus on her face. Everything was blurry.

"Y-You came to see us the other night, didn't you?" The words made sense in my head, but I wasn't sure whether my dry tongue conveyed them properly. She smiled. I couldn't see her smile, not underneath that mask covering most of her face, but her eyes smiled. Her dark, angry eyes.

"It'll come back to you, with time," she said.

"With... what?" She wasn't making any sense. The stench of blood assaulted my nostrils and sickness rose in my stomach. "It was you, wasn't it?"

She said nothing. She didn't have to. The trench coat killer wasn't hiding herself from me because she didn't have to. She wanted me to know. The only thing I couldn't figure out was... why.

"Who are you? Why are you doing this?"

She raised the knife and I flinched, waiting for it to pierce my skin. Bring an end to my sorry life. Only it didn't. She wiped it clean on my shirt and then placed it in my hands.

"You'll see. You'll remember."

I looked down at the knife, confused. She turned and walked away, stepping over Jo's dead body and making her way back down the road.

"Hey! Wait!"

Footsteps sounded nearby. Someone was coming. I panicked. I was covered in blood, holding a knife, and standing over a dead body.

I ran. I ran as fast as my legs would carry me, as far from Rakucho as I could possibly get.

16

SEVERAL MESSAGES FROM KOJI AWAITED me as I opened my phone. The knife stared at me from the kitchen counter, the image of it placed between Jo's teeth burned into my mind. I could hear him screaming, begging for help as she plunged the knife in, over and over.

I shook my head. No. He was already dead by then.

Except he wasn't. He was still breathing.

But he never said anything. He just... gurgled.

Only he did scream. I could hear it, clear as day.

I grabbed a beer from the fridge and downed it. It spilt over my chin and down my neck. Droplets fell to the floor and mixed with the blood on my clothes. When it was done I doubled over, coughing, and grabbed another.

The screaming wouldn't stop. The knife, going in, over and over, slicing through flesh like butter each time. He was screaming, crying, pleading for his life. I did nothing.

I sat on the couch and turned the TV on. I flicked through the channels for a few minutes, fighting the desire to see whether his body had been found yet. No doubt it had. He wasn't exactly hidden, lying on the grass in the open like that.

My heart flipped and my stomach churned. Were my fingerprints on him? How long was I passed out for? What did she do while I was out? Had she... I shook my head. Images flashed through my mind, but nothing made sense. Nothing.

Narumi, if you're gonna leave early for the night, at least let us know. The boss is livid.

Koji. I could talk to Koji. I couldn't take it to Yotchan. Koji was the only person I could tell. He would know who the woman was. He knew everything that went on at the club. Yes. Koji.

Koji. We need to talk.

I hit send and closed my eyes. The fury as the woman stabbed Jo in the grass, gurgling and choking on his own blood, terrified me. The look as she placed the knife between his teeth, like she was grinning, and the smile as she handed the knife to me.

I had to get rid of it. I couldn't just throw it away. It was covered in my fingerprints, and even if I wiped it clean, there was no way to guarantee that my DNA wasn't still hidden on it somewhere.

I could stash it. Hide it behind the washing machine, or stick it behind the drawers in the kitchen. Nobody would ever find it there. It would be gone, and with it, any evidence linking me to the crimes I hadn't committed.

"Why didn't you save me?" I grabbed another beer, pushing the voice out of my head. "I was right there. You heard me. I was alive. A few steps and you could have saved me. Why didn't you save me?"

"Shut up, shut up!" I threw the remote at the wall. Police were lining an area with tape on the TV. The text was blurry… everything was blurry… but I recognised it well enough. They had already found Jo's body. He was the third victim of what they were calling the Rakucho Nightcrawler. They didn't even know it was a woman. They didn't know anything.

"We were buddies, weren't we?" The voice continued. "Workmates. Comrades. How could you leave a comrade to die?"

"I didn't even know you that well!" I screamed. I looked around my apartment, knowing full well that I was alone, but searching for the source of the voice, regardless.

"Of course you did. We've worked together for a while now. I looked up to you. Learnt from you. We hosts gotta stick together, but instead, you let me die."

"What was I supposed to do?" I was talking to myself. There was no voice. No spirit. Jo wasn't haunting my apartment. That was stupid. There was no such thing as ghosts. It was all in my head. My drunken head that was unable to process the images it saw. I closed my eyes and let the bitter liquid spill down my face again as I attempted to lose myself in it.

"How could you let me die?"

I refused to answer. It wasn't real. It was in my head. It was the shock talking. I opened my eyes. Jo was standing in front of me, his jaw lolling where the woman had nearly severed right through. His cheeks stretched, the pulpy flesh pulling apart like cheese.

"You did this." His voice, unnatural and deep, boomed. Blood poured out of the stab wounds in his chest, spilling over the floor and mixing with the beer. I closed my eyes and covered my ears.

"You're just a figment of my imagination. None of this is real. It's just shock. I'm still drunk. None of this is real…"

The metallic tang of iron reached my nostrils. My hands grew warm. I opened my eyes, and they were covered in blood again. Only this time, I was holding the knife, and it was pressed deep into Jo's heart.

"You did this!"

I let go and fell back. He was gone. The knife clattered to the floor. The otherwise clean floor with nothing but beer on it. I looked around. I was alone. All alone. My hands were clean, no blood on them. I patted myself and checked my face and shirt and arms. Nothing there.

Just my imagination. I let out the breath I didn't realise I'd been holding. Pushing myself to my feet, I stumbled over to the knife and picked it up. My heart caught in my throat.

Blood. It was covered in blood. I let go of it and it clattered to the floor again. I grabbed some tissues and wiped it clean. It wasn't mine; I had no injuries nor was I bleeding anywhere. I flushed the bloody tissues down the toilet and threw the knife into the bottom drawer. I didn't want to touch it or even see it again. Jo's words echoed in my mind.

"You did this."

17

KOJI GRIMACED AS I CAME stumbling into the club. Haruki sat at the main couch with a woman on each side of him. Music blared, drinks poured, and laughter filled the room. He was having the time of his life and apparently unaffected by everything else going on around us. He didn't see her. He didn't know the fear, the pain, the worry that he might be next. He was too stupid for that. That needed to be fixed.

"What on earth happened to you? The boss is going to flay your ass when he sees you!"

"Koji, shut up, listen! I need help!"

He gave me the once over and screwed up his face. "Yeah, no shit. When was the last time you slept?"

"Yesterday." Technically it was the truth. The best truth. "That's not important. You remember that woman, right?"

Koji finished cleaning some glasses and turned

to put them back on the shelf. I grabbed one and filled it from the tap myself.

"What woman? And Narumi, are you sure that's the best idea right now?"

"Absolutely." I took a big swig. My last drink was half an hour earlier. I'd run out at home. Here, it was free. Technically. And the more I drank the less I saw *him*. Just had to keep him at bay. Did they already know? They had to. Yet everyone was carrying on like... "And I mean the woman. The one who was in here the other night. You know?"

"You'll need to be a little more specific." He frowned at me. He could frown all he wanted. I intended to make it out of this alive.

"The one with the mask! We even spoke about her!"

"Mizuki?"

"Yes! Her!" I knew I could count on Koji. "I need to know everything you can tell me about her. Everything." I looked around the room, my hand trembling as it clenched the glass pressed to my lips. Even fewer hosts than usual, but no signs that any of them knew Jo was the latest victim. Maybe they thought he'd chosen to skip out as well.

"Hey Narumi!" Haruki's deep voice rang out across the room. Anger bubbled in my stomach. I wasn't ready to deal with him, not right now.

"What?"

He gestured for me to come over. The women beside him giggled. Koji shrugged. I took another drink and walked over.

"So, the ladies and I are trying to settle something. A little bet, if you will." He snorted as he tried—badly—to stop a laugh from escaping.

"And what's that?"

One of the women leaned forward and raised a hand to cover her mouth. "We wanted to know how old you really are." She broke into giggles and her friend joined her.

"I'm telling you, he's in his 40s," the other woman said. "I'm into older men, I can tell these things. Mid-40s at least."

Her friend shook her head. "No, no, you don't understand. I've seen this happen with my older brother. He drinks a lot because of work and is always sleep deprived. He's gotta be late-30s at best."

Haruki raised his eyebrows and grinned. "Settle the debate for the ladies, would you? Loser has to shout all drinks for the next hour."

I clenched my fist and turned to walk away.

"Hey! There's no need to be rude!"

I stopped in my tracks. Koji shook his head. He could already see what was coming. I pivoted on the spot, leaned down, and grabbed one of their drinks from the table. I swallowed it in a single gulp, letting the champagne dribble down my chin. The women grimaced in disgust.

"You did this."

I shook my head. The young host on standby in the corner turned to me. Only it wasn't the young host anymore. It was Jo. Blood stained his shirt, grass and dirt stuck to the blood on his face, and trickles of red liquid started running down his cheeks, like he was smiling, but his lips weren't moving.

"I did nothing!" I screamed. "It wasn't my fault!"

Haruki furrowed his brow. "What?"

"She's going to keep killing. You know it and you let her."

"No!"

"Because you want her to. Because you like it." The bloody former-host stepped towards me, the line of blood spreading up towards his ears as the flesh of his cheeks tore. "Less competition for yourself, right?"

"That's not it!"

"You want us dead. You're why we're dead. You killed us. You took the knife and plunged it into our—"

"No!" I threw the champagne glass at him. It hit the wall and shattered. When I looked back up, the host's eyes were wide open in fear. There was no blood. No dirt or grass on him. There was just a shattered glass on the floor, alcohol dripping down the wall, and a terrified young host looking back at me. Haruki stood up, and the women cowered behind him.

"What the fuck is wrong with you?"

Koji came running over from behind the bar, but it was too late. Haruki reached out to grab my shirt, and I grabbed the champagne bottle from the table. I swung, colliding with a solid thunk as it hit his head. The women screamed and two more guys ran over to break up the fight.

"I didn't do anything!" I grabbed Haruki's shirt and swung a fist at his face. He was taller and more muscular than me, but the combined rage and fear fuelled me. Plus, hitting him felt *good*. How long had I waited to do this? Too long. Far too long.

Haruki grabbed me around the midsection and charged forward, right past Koji and into the bar. My back slammed into the edge, knocking the wind from me. Another of the guys grabbed my fist as I raised it to hit Haruki again.

"Narumi! Stop!"

I yanked my wrist free, grabbed a glass from the table, and smashed it into his face instead. Blood trickled to the ground as he stumbled back.

"I did nothing!"

Haruki grabbed my hair and pushed my face down into the bar. "Don't make me hurt you, old man," he growled. A thin stream of blood trickled down from his temple. Jo smiled at me from the corner, the top half of his head lolling back from his split jaw. It was as though he was laughing so hard that his head was falling off from the hilarity of it all. I squeezed my eyes shut. The music in the bar reverberated through the wood. Voices screamed over the top of each other, trying to gain dominance. Pressure in my head built as the cold bar cooled my cheeks. Someone tugged at my free hand. Then it all stopped. Like someone had pulled the plug.

They had. It was the boss.

"What on earth is going on down here?"

Haruki released me and straightened up, breathing heavily. A drop of blood landed on his shoulder. He wavered, but remained upright.

"I—"

"Narumi just had a little too much to drink

tonight, it would seem," Koji interjected. "I think we can all agree that it's been a rough few days. For all of us." He looked pointedly at me. "Shut up," his eyes screamed. "Don't make this any worse."

"Narumi!"

I stood up and brushed off my shirt. "Yes, sir?"

"Did you do all this?"

The skin around his eyes darkened. The white of his eyes filled in with red. Multiple holes in his chest gushed blood and then a thin line appeared on his neck, starting from his left ear and ending at his right. I closed my eyes and shook my head. When I opened them again, it was all gone.

"Haruki and I were just having a friendly chat." I tried to grin, but I could feel my eye swelling and I tasted blood. My own blood.

"A friendly chat? You smashed my property, caused a ruckus in my bar, and frightened my customers, all for a friendly chat?"

I flinched as his voice rose. You could hear a pin drop, the bar was so quiet. Nobody said a word. Nobody moved a muscle. The boss said something to the women, bowing profusely and handing each of them a card. They quickly shuffled out of the bar and he turned back to unleash his full wrath upon us.

"Get out of here."

"What?" His words threw me. I was expecting more anger, more berating, more "imbecile, what have you done?"

"Get out. Don't come back until you've gotten your shit together. If I see you drunk in here again, you're fired, do you hear me?" Silence. "Do you hear me?" I jumped at the sudden raise in his voice.

"Y-Yes, sir."

"Good. Now get out. Clean yourself up, and I better not see any of this again when you come back. You're on thin ice here, I don't care how long we've known each other. This behaviour is unacceptable. I think you need to start seriously considering whether this is the job for you anymore." He surveyed the club once more. "I know you don't like it, but it might be time to consider retirement. Find something else to do." He turned to Koji. "Clean this up. The rest of you, get to work. We're going to need even more customers to cover the cost of all this now. Hit the streets." He gave me one last look before disappearing into the back room. The anger from his eyes was gone, replaced with something else. Pity. Disappointment. Sadness.

"Narumi—"

I grabbed a glass from the bar, finished the dregs and held my hand up.

"Not now."

I pulled myself up the stairs and pushed out into the humidity of Rakucho. My head pounded and the ache in my shoulder flared up.

Now what?

18

After wandering around Rakucho for several hours, I found myself in front of another Family Cart. The doorbell tinkled as I entered and a deadpan voice greeted me. I stumbled past the rows of magazines and face packs and into the toilet. The contents of my stomach relieved themselves, splashing all over the rim. The mirror shunned me, casting light so bright that it seemed like it was trying to drive me away with blindness.

"Ugh." I looked like shit. I washed my face and rivulets of water dripped into the sink. My right eye was thankfully not too swollen, just a small bruise forming on the outside. My lip was split, although it had already closed. Neither of those contributed to my overall look of death, however.

"What a waste of money…" The face packs had done nothing for my skin. The wrinkles were as deep as ever, the lines boring into my face like rivers on a map. The voices of the women joking about my age clenched around my heart and squeezed, choking me of whatever life I had left. My rank was dropping even further at the club, and my bank account was rapidly drying out. Fewer women wanted to go out with me after work, and my line of credit had been halted. Now I'd been kicked out of work for a fight I didn't even start.

The writing was on the wall, but I didn't have to accept it. That was what quitters did, not the top salesmen in their business. I was, after all, a salesman, and I was very good at what I did. I was the product, and I sold a fantasy that gave women a getaway from the horrors of reality. That boring place where their husbands spent all night at work and bars; that place where kids nagged them day in, day out; that place where they didn't have any close friends anymore, because everyone had drifted apart and hey, that was life. I sold excitement, I sold thrills, I sold a feeling that women couldn't get at home anymore and that, well, that was priceless. But if you were a salesman and you found a fault in your main product line, you didn't scrap the entire line and move onto something different. You fixed the fault and continued working with the brand that had brought you fame and recognition.

I stumbled out of the toilet and squinted in the bright lights of the convenience store. The doorbell tinkled as a young couple exited, laughing and spilling their beer into the street.

"Thank you for shopping at Family Cart..." the cashier's dead voice followed them out the door. I grabbed a beer from the fridge and a vitamin drink from beside the cashier and threw a note down.

"That'll be 450 yen…"

The cashier handed me the change on autopilot and I opened the can before I was out the door. Everything would be okay now. All of this was just a minor setback.

"Thank you for shopping at Family Cart…"

There was no need to give up the lifestyle I'd grown accustomed to over the last 20 years. I had a very particular skill set that I'd honed and I was, quite frankly, the best at what I did. So some newer models had come in that were newer and shinier, so what? I allowed that to blind me, and that was my fault. They couldn't do what I could. They didn't know what I did. I let myself go and, yes, that was my fault. But no longer. I pulled out my phone.

Someone laughed behind me. I spun around, but the street was empty. "Hello?"

"You really are something, aren't you?"

Behind me again. I spun. Nothing.

"What do you want?"

"You know that's not the answer to your problem."

I turned and stood face to face with Jo. That familiar metallic tang invaded my nostrils and threatened to bring whatever was left in my stomach back up. I shook my head.

"You're not real."

"So you keep telling yourself. Yet here I am."

"You're just a figment of my imagination."

"Even if I am, that doesn't change the fact that I'm right."

I threw the can at him. It flew past him and landed in the gutter with a small thud, spilling its contents out into the street. A group of kids stopped as they were turning the corner and looked at me. They were all in blue.

"You gotta problem, old man?" a big kid in front said.

"I don't have time for this..." I turned the other way and started walking. Footsteps caught up behind me.

"Hey, hey, now that's not very polite. You try to injure *us*, some innocent kids out for a night of fun, and then you walk away without even saying sorry?"

I grabbed the kid's jacket and yanked him. "I really don't have the time for this right now. You get it?" I pushed him off me and he laughed. He stepped back into the throng of teens behind him and motioned with his right hand. They rushed forward and jumped me, a hurricane of punches and kicks beating me into the ground. I covered my face as their fists and feet found their mark. Somewhere I heard a voice, and laughter, and I realised it wasn't the blue leader. It was *him*.

"Look at you. Pathetic. At least I put up a fight when I died. When they find you, they're just gonna find a sad sack of washed up flesh."

Fists pounded my face, my shoulders, my back. My head swam in and out. I waited for the darkness to claim me, but I wasn't to be so lucky. They stopped suddenly and then stepped back. The leader knelt down before me, holding something. My phone.

"Even your phone is ancient, geez. Free tip, old man, because you look like you could use it.

Rakucho belongs to us now. Go entertain your little old ladies elsewhere. You're not wanted here anymore. And look next time before you decide to trash our beautiful city. You might hit someone." He dropped the phone on my face and laughed, disappearing into the darkness with his gang. I sat up and grabbed my head. Furious throbbing threatened to once again expel what little stomach contents I had, but I pushed it back down. I grabbed my phone and opened the camera to look at myself. A tiny cut on my forehead, but my face was otherwise unharmed. Thank god. My arms and stomach were sore and tender, but that didn't matter. As long as my face was fine.

"Little shits. They'll get what's coming to them…"

"And what's that?" Jo chimed in again. "You gonna kill them too?"

I ignored him. Crawling over to the gutter, I sat down and dialled. I wasn't sure if anyone would answer, so I was surprised when the other end picked up.

"Smiling Bright. How may I help you?"

I knew that voice. It was Dr Nakata.

"Hi, yes, um, I came in for a free consultation recently and…"

"Ah yes, Narumi?"

I laughed. How did he remember my name so quickly?

"Y-Yes, that's right."

"Have you thought things over?"

"…I have."

"Excellent! And?"

"How soon can you fit me in?"

There was a brief silence followed by tapping on a keyboard. I could almost hear him smiling on the other end.

"We have several slots open this weekend, although if you'd prefer a weekday—"

"The weekend sounds great," I said. "What's the soonest you have?"

"How does Saturday at one sound?"

"In the afternoon?"

He laughed. "Yes, I'm not in the habit of working quite so late into the night, unlike yourself. Although, admittedly, my hours are flexible for clients such as yourself who can't make it any other time."

"One in the afternoon sounds perfect. Doctor?"

"Yes?"

"Can you really help me?"

A brief silence. "Of course."

Why the pause? Was the pause really necessary? Was there something he wasn't telling me?

"Okay. Yeah, sure, of course. I'll uh, see you then."

"Wonderful! Until then."

I hung up. Just a small procedure. Just had to get rid of the wrinkles. That was all. Then everything would go back to how it always was.

I would be number one again.

19

I NEEDED A SHOWER AND rest, but I didn't want to go home. I would be all alone there, and then *he* would bother me even more, but I couldn't exactly hang around on the streets.

"Welcome!"

The receptionist of the Blissful Nights capsule hotel greeted me as I stepped inside. I had used it a handful of times over the years, and it was decent enough for the price. The carpet smelt kinda bad, and the walls were a little sticky, but you could do worse.

"Hi. Just looking to stay for a couple of hours," I said, grinning. Pain tore through my lip. My attempts at hiding it were apparently unsuccessful.

"Sir... are you okay?"

"Fine. Just tripped over outside. Drinking too much. You know how it goes." I continued to force the smile. It hurt like hell.

"Yeah... sure." She typed a few things into her

computer and then handed me a key. "Fifth floor. Capsules are in numerical order. Showers are on the third floor, toilets on every second floor. If you need anything else, the front desk is open 24 hours."

I smiled and grabbed the key. "Thank you." The elevator was waiting on the sixth floor. I took the stairs instead and went straight to the third. My knees creaked and ached. My head throbbed. My shoulder wouldn't stop nagging me. I had no change of clothes, but at the very least, a shower was better than nothing. As I took my shirt off, I noticed all the cuts and bruises the blues had given me, as well as the little pouch of belly fat hanging over my pants. I sighed. Gym could fix that. It wasn't the worst problem in the world. I could use a little more exercise, anyway. Movement kept the body young, or so they said.

The water was cold. That was fine. Outside was so humid that it was refreshing. I finished up and got back into my dirty clothes. Better than nothing. My stomach grumbled and I realised I hadn't eaten all night. My eyelids drooped and it was hard to focus. I climbed the stairs, found my room, and crawled in. Just a short nap. Food could wait.

It was after 8 when I woke. I sat up and hit my head on the roof of the capsule. "Shit." I only meant to lie down for an hour or two. My stomach grumbled loudly. "Yeah, yeah." I crawled out and grabbed my phone. There was a single message from Koji.

"You okay?"

I put the phone in my pocket and went downstairs.

"Did you hear?"

"Hear what?"

The receptionist was talking to another woman, perhaps her shift change.

"They found another body last night!"

"What? No way!"

She nodded. "They were just talking about it on the news. The Rakucho Nightcrawler strikes again!"

The other woman screwed up her face. "Who was it? Another host?"

Her friend nodded.

"If I were them, I'd get out of town. Quick."

"I know, right? No amount of money can be worth that."

"Speaking of money, I heard some guys talking outside before. Apparently the body they found was that of the number one host!"

My heart stopped.

"No way!"

"Uh huh."

"He really is getting brazen. That's, what, three in one week? I wonder why he's killing them. Hosts, I mean."

The woman shrugged. "Revenge? It's always revenge, isn't it? Maybe the guy found his wife spending all his money on hosts so he's killing them."

"No way. Oh, maybe it's another host! Maybe he got kicked out, or maybe he got sick of seeing everyone else make money and now he's picking them off, one by one, until he's the only one left!"

Her friend laughed. "That's stupid. Why would a host do that? Nobody wants to visit one of those clubs if everyone's getting murdered. Oh! It's gotta be a rival business owner! That's it! He's trying to make all those clubs look bad so people will start flocking to his business instead!"

The number one host was dead? Haruki? No. He couldn't be. I was with him last night. We fought. We... fought.

"Hi." I smiled and the two women turned to look at me.

"Oh! I'm terribly sorry! I didn't realise you were waiting."

I shook my hand. "No, it's fine. I just got here. If you don't mind my asking, you said that they found another body last night?"

The women exchanged glances and then looked me over once more.

"Yes..."

"Did they happen to say who it was? Something about the number one host?"

Both ladies remained silent. A silent conversation was taking place about whether they should say anything to me, a host standing right before them... and not a very clean one at that. Finally the woman sitting at the computer spoke.

"That's what I heard, yes. Why, have you heard anything about what's going on? Is someone really targeting hosts?" She turned the questions on me in an instant, her curiosity getting the better of her.

"I know as much as you do." I shrugged. "This number one guy, did they describe him?"

She shook her head. "I just saw it on the news, and they didn't show anything."

"I see." Koji. I had to talk to him. He would

know. "Thank you." I handed the key over and both women bowed their heads.

"Thank you for staying with Blissful Nights!" they echoed in unison as I stepped out into the street. The morning was oddly cool and quiet. I dialled Koji but there was no answer. He was probably asleep. Maybe he hadn't even heard yet.

The boss. He would still be at the club. Hell, I wasn't sure if he even had a home to go to, he was always there. If it was Haruki, there was no way he wouldn't know about it. After Jo, the police would have to take that to him.

And if it *was* Haruki? Emotions stirred up within me. He was my rival, yes, and he was a shithead, yes, but I didn't wish him dead. I just wanted him gone. Out of my hair. Never wanted to see him again. There was a difference between disliking a person and wanting them gone and hoping for that person to actually die. I wasn't a monster. Not even he deserved that. But if it was him, then that meant...

I started running.

20

A LARGE SIGN AFFIXED TO the front of Club Tenshi stated *CLOSED*. I banged on the door several times, but there was no answer. How the hell was the club closed? Why? It was too sudden. Nothing made sense.

"Hello?" I screamed. The door was solid wood with no window to speak of, so peeking through it was impossible. Just how most host clubs preferred it. No point having the law sneaking glances, and if a customer wanted to know more, getting them inside hugely increased chances of them staying. It was simple business sense. Now, however, it infuriated me. "Hello?"

Nothing. I went around to the back exit. Padlocked. Neither that nor the piece of wood hanging by the front door were good signs. Grabbing my phone, I dialled the boss. After a few rings, someone answered.

"What?"

"Boss! It's me! Narumi! Thank god."

"Narumi?" His voice hesitated a moment. "You're okay?"

"Of course I'm okay. Why wouldn't I be?"

Silence. A voice muttered something in the background and the boss covered the phone as he replied. Probably his wife. "Where are you?" he asked.

"Standing in front of Club Tenshi. There's a closed sign out the front. Are you really...?"

Another brief silence before he cleared his throat and spoke in that gruff tone that meant no nonsense. "Narumi, I think you should go home. Lie low for a while, you get me? Seriously think about where you want to go from here."

"Go home? Are you serious? You're actually closing the club? Over a few murders around town?"

"Haruki's dead."

My heart stopped.

"I'm sorry, come again?"

"He's dead, Narumi. So is Jo. I thought that maybe he'd skipped out for the night with everything that's been going on, but... Look, I need to go down to the station shortly to give my statement, and they're going to be calling you shortly as well. I sure as hell hope for your sake that you have a good reason for your absence last night."

"My... what?" Was he implying I had something to do with it? I shook my head and planted a hand on the door before me.

"Boss, listen, I'm not following. Break it down for me."

"Narumi, just get home. Get some sleep."

"No, wait, listen, you can't just close the club. I... I need that money." At this rate I would be kicked out of my apartment soon. No work meant no place to live. No place to live meant no work. No work meant no women, no fun, no anything. "You can't close the club. Are you insane?"

"Go home, Narumi."

"No!" I screamed. "You can't do this! I need to work! I need that money!"

"They're dead!" the boss screamed back. He didn't often get worked up, and for a moment I was taken aback. "Do you hear me? They're dead. This is about more than your money, boy."

In my panic, all I could see was my life ending before my eyes. It was tragic, yes, but why should their loss impact my job and right to live?

"You can't—"

"I'm hanging up now."

"No, wait!" I scratched the back of my head. Sweat poured down my brow in the harsh sunlight of morning. It was an unusual hour for me to be awake, and I didn't like it. "Couldn't you just... I dunno, let me in for the night, or—"

"Get some sleep. Don't come in until I call you. Better yet, take this time to think things over, okay?" He hung up.

Closed. Club Tenshi was closed until further notice. Jo and Haruki, the number one and two respectively of our club were dead. It didn't seem real. Haruki... My rival. He was punching me in the face less than 12 hours ago, and now he was gone? Just like that? It was too sudden. It didn't make any sense. Maybe they made a mistake? Maybe it was another host that looked like Haruki? Maybe Haruki had gone into hiding and when they couldn't find him they assumed that the body was his. It couldn't be him. He was a raging douchebag and I hated him with every fibre of my being, but that didn't mean I wanted him dead...

My stomach grumbled and sweat stuck to my already sticky clothes. My shoulder ached and a small stabbing pain in my knee was driving me nuts. Sobriety and sunlight wasn't all it was cracked up to be. And as tragic as Haruki and Jo's deaths were, they had presented me with yet another problem on their way out: how was I going to make money now? Maybe I could get work at another club? Sure, it was pathetic, but it was less pathetic than being kicked out of home and going hungry because someone else decided to take my livelihood away. I was still one of the highest ranked hosts in Rakucho, anyone would be lucky to have me.

A figured wavered in the distance. It seemed to dance in the heat waves, its arms out to its side, waving as its body jerked to and fro. I rubbed my eyes and squinted against the light. It was coming closer.

"What the fuck?"

I looked around, but I was the only one there. The wavering figure stumbled closer and closer. The waves of heat rising from the road baking in the morning sunlight made it even more difficult to see through already blurry eyes. I placed a hand above my eyes to shield from the sunlight and squinted. It was most definitely coming towards me, and with each wobble it seemed to get faster. Those clothes... Was that... Haruki?

"Shit."

I ran behind the back of the building and nestled beside the dumpster. Before long the sound of something scraping along the asphalt reached me ears. It was close. What the hell was it? It sounded like... it was dragging its feet? Or it had a limp. Either way, it was dragging something, and the sound was growing louder by the moment. It couldn't be Haruki. That made no sense. The clothes and general shape looked similar through the blistering waves of heat, but lots of people dressed like that. No, it wasn't him. It couldn't be. Why would he be dragging himself down the middle of the street in broad daylight if the police said they had his body?

Just pass by. Keep going. I'm not here and I don't want anything to do with whatever you are. My brain screamed the words, attempting to wish them into reality through pure force of will alone. I clenched my eyes shut and pushed myself back into the shadows. The sound of my heartbeat was going to give me away, I knew it.

Dragging. Wobbling. Getting closer.

Go away.

It was by the side of the building. The sound stopped. It was searching.

Keep going. You don't want anything to do with me. Go.

The dragging started again. Good. That's it. Keep going.

Beep beep. Beep beep.

Shit! My phone!

The dragging stopped. My hand found its way to my pocket, waiting with bated breath for it to go off again. It didn't. It was just a message. I didn't realise it wasn't on silent. If another message came, however…

Dragging. This time towards me. It heard. It knew I was there. It was all over. I was trapped between a wall and a dumpster. Just a few more metres until it would be in front of me and I really had nowhere to go.

What was it? Why was it coming for me? Why was all of this happening now? I just wanted to live a quiet life, keep doing what I was good at, and then retire at a ripe old age when I was good and ready. I couldn't do that if I died next to a giant trash can hidden in the back alleys of Rakucho. Someone would find my mangled body, sure, but not before it had been cooking in the summer heat for most of the day, leaving me bloated and noxious, flesh sloughing off my bones when the police finally came to collect the rotting remains. "Ugh," they would say. "We found another one. Phew, sure wouldn't want to have been this guy in his final moments. Whaddaya say we get some yakiniku after this? What? Too soon?"

No. I wasn't dying in a random back alley so my corpse could bloat and rot and explode in the heat. I wasn't dying to some weird wobbling creature that nobody else seemed to see in the broad daylight. Nor was I going to die to some woman in a trench coat wielding a knife and picking off my colleagues one by one.

Not today!
Feet dragged just a few metres away.
I screamed and ran.

21

No looking back. If I turned back, I would see it, and if I saw it, it would see me, and if it saw me, it would all be over. My feet pounded the hot pavement and I ran without direction. Something was very, very wrong with Rakucho. What next, headless riders? Rokurokubi? Super-fast grannies?

Finally reaching the large red arch leading into Rakucho, I stopped beneath it to catch my breath. Fitness was not my forte. Perhaps a few more visits to the gym with Yotchan wouldn't be a bad idea after all.

Yotchan.

I pulled out my phone and dialled. It rang and rang and then rang some more. "Dammit!" I hung up in frustration. Where the hell was he? A familiar face nearby waved. Mitsuhiro, the taxi driver.

"You're out late," he said, winding his window down. "Need a lift?"

I nodded, unsure of what else to do. Was the

thing behind me in the crowd? Was it lurking in the shadows, waiting for my return? All I had to do was turn back to see. That would confirm everything.

The taxi door opened. I got in without turning around. "Let's go."

"Rough night?"

I nodded.

"I heard another host was killed last night."

I nodded again.

"Is everything okay."

I shook my head. Mitsuhiro adjusted his mirror and fell silent for a moment. "Sir, if I may, perhaps it would be best if you spent a few nights away from Rakucho. Just in case."

"That's what everyone keeps telling me..." I muttered. He tried to smile, shifting in his seat to get more comfortable.

"Think of it as a vacation! Surely there's somewhere you'd love to be right now?"

Come to think of it, there wasn't. It hit me that I had zero desires outside being the number one host of Rakucho. I had dedicated my entire life to it, at the expense of everything else. No wife, no kids, no family. No hobbies. Nothing that didn't help me in my goal of becoming number one. Was I really that boring? That wasn't to say I hadn't travelled; I'd been all over, often with clients as sort of extended dates.

"How are your kids, Mitsuhiro?" I changed the subject. It wasn't something I wished to dwell on.

"Fine, sir. Thank you for asking."

"And the wife?"

"Same old, same old." He smiled. I tried to smile

back, but no doubt my face betrayed my real emotions. We drove the rest of the way in silence.

"Here we are," Mitsuhiro said as he pulled in in front of my apartment building. "This one's on me. Try to get some rest, and perhaps take a break for a few days, yes?"

I nodded and thanked him. He waved as he pulled out and disappeared down the road. I turned to look up both sides of the street. Nothing wobbling. Nothing dragging. Nothing waving. No woman in a trench coat. No bloody face screaming at me to save him. Nothing but me and some searing big city heat.

And a lack of things to drink.

The notes in my wallet were rapidly dwindling. Just a few drinks from the nearby convenience store would tide me over. I grabbed a six pack, plopped it on the counter and slid over a note. The cashier wordlessly handed me the change. "Thank you for shopping at Family Cart," echoed faintly as the door closed behind me. I opened the first can and let the liquid sting my throat. I pulled out a cigarette, squatted by the bins, and closed my eyes.

"You didn't even stop to see what it was."

My heart dropped. I squeezed my eyes shut and took another drink.

"It could have been someone who needed help. Someone like me. Or *him*."

"Go away."

"I wouldn't be here if you hadn't done this to me in the first place."

I took a drag of the cigarette and let it fill my lungs for a moment.

"What, can't even look at me now? Why doesn't that surprise me? Running from your problems, that's all you're good at."

"You're not real." I took another drink.

"Says who? You? You're not exactly the most reliable source around, you know."

A metallic tang filled my nostrils. He was right by my face. I could reach out and choke him... if he were real. I blew smoke instead. He coughed.

"You're scared, aren't you?"

"Of what?"

He laughed. "Of everything. You've spent your entire life avoiding being an adult, avoiding any type of responsibility whatsoever. Now everything is being shaken up and you're afraid."

I opened my eyes. Blood poured from the wounds in his chest and his jaw lolled as a hot breeze blew. I didn't bother asking how he could talk with his mouth like that. He wasn't real. He could do whatever he wanted.

"Yeah, I'm afraid. Afraid of dying."

"Like me."

"Like you."

He smiled. Or at least, he attempted to smile. Blood dripped onto my jeans.

"You're not going to make it out of this alive, you know?" I finished the can and threw it in the trash. "You'll get what's coming to you. What you deserve."

"And what's that?" My voice came out angrier than I intended, but this persistent figment of my imagination was getting on my nerves. Jo placed a finger by the side of my mouth and drew upwards.

Warmth and wetness followed. He placed it by the other side and repeated the action. Then he smiled. The bottom half of his jaw wavered like a broken toy lid. He continued laughing, throwing his head back, and then he rushed me in an instant. I jumped back into the convenience store window, his nose just millimetres from mine.

"Soon," he growled, and then he was gone. My heart pounded in my chest as it rose and fell. I closed my eyes and shook my head. It was stress. The stress of everything was making me see things. It would all be over soon. I'd visit the doc, get that sorted out, a few more gym visits with Yotchan would straighten everything else out, and once this trench coat woman was finally caught, then work would go back to normal as well. As horrible as it sounded, with less competition for me as well.

I took a deep breath to calm myself and slowly released it. A couple holding hands walked by. I grinned. The woman stopped and pointed at me.

"Uh, you have something on your face, sir."

Her boyfriend quickly pulled her into the store. I turned to look in the windows, my face reflected back in the light. Streaks of blood marred my cheeks, spreading up from my lips in a horrific grin.

In the distance, someone laughed.

22

I WIPED THE BLOOD OFF my face and threw the bloody rag in the trash. The look of fear in the young couple's eyes as they pointed at me struck deep. It wasn't a look I was used to. People looked up to me, people respected me, and people loved me. They didn't fear me. They didn't pity me. I didn't like it. Not one little bit.

The couch groaned as I sat on it. I lit a cigarette and then opened another can of beer. I didn't even want to drink it, but what choice did I have? The liquid, what once tasted like sweet life-giving waters as it went down my throat, now tasted bitter and harsh. Many long years of drinking alcohol had both given me a high tolerance to it and also ruined my liver. I wasn't well, and I knew it, but I couldn't stop myself.

Something on the TV muttered in the background. I wasn't watching it. I coughed after blowing some smoke out and then lay my head back, closing my eyes. This was a new level of tired. I had known exhaustion; been best friends with it for many years, even. One didn't reach the top through sheer luck; it was achieved through many years of hard work and doing what others weren't willing to. This, however, was different. I feared that closing my eyes meant I would never open them again.

"Maybe you won't."

Adrenaline coursed through my body. I clenched my eyes tightly and took another drink.

"Maybe it would be better for us all if you didn't open your eyes again. Maybe I would still be here."

Just ignore him. He's already had his fun for tonight. Just ignore him and he'll go away.

"But I won't go away. You did this to me, Narumi. You. You're the reason I'm stuck here, unable to move on, and you better believe that I'm not going anywhere."

"What did I do?" I screamed, throwing my can against the wall. Sticky liquid splashed all over the TV and then dribbled down. He laughed. I couldn't see him, but I could hear him. He was all around me, first in this ear and then the next.

"You know, we all looked up to you."

I spun around, but I was alone. Completely and utterly alone. "Who did?"

"Us. All of us. The hosts you got killed."

"What are you talking about?" I was going crazy. That was it. Stress had finally gotten to me. I laughed. "I didn't kill anyone!"

"Is that so?" A familiar voice, yet different to the first, sounded by my right ear.

CHAPTER TWENTY-TWO

"…Haruki?"

"Didn't expect me to find you here, huh?"

I stood up and spun around. Nobody was in the room. It was just me. "Haruki, I don't, I didn't—"

"But that's the problem, isn't it, Narumi? You don't ever do anything. Nothing's ever your fault. It's not your fault you lost the top spot, is it? No, that was all our fault."

"I never—"

"And it wasn't your fault that your clients started to move over not just to me, but to Jo, and even other clubs as well, was it?"

"I didn't know—"

"Of course, it was never your fault that you couldn't remember all your customers' names, was it? I mean, there were just so many, who could be expected to remember something as small and insignificant as the name of the person who paid for your livelihood, who allowed you to live the life of your dreams, am I right?"

Another voice mumbled words of acknowledgement by my left ear. I didn't know whether the voice really was Haruki, or just something pretending to be him… Or just something inside my head. But did it really matter? The result was the same.

"I did nothing," I repeated. "I did nothing!"

"And that brings us to the crux of the situation, doesn't it, Narumi?" The other voice. Jo. I spun around, again and again, but still I was alone. Soft sunlight filtered through the curtains and the room stank of alcohol and smoke. I said nothing. "You never do anything, do you? Or so you like to tell yourself. Look deep, Narumi."

"Look deep," Haruki agreed. I spun and was met with more nothingness.

"At what?" My voice grew hoarse. "Look deep at what? You're not making any sense! You're not even real!" I sat back down on the couch, took a deep breath, and steadied my hand. Ash fell to the carpet, but that was the least of my concerns. The voices were just in my head. Stress. They were nothing more than the result of the stressful surroundings I found myself in. Once things got back to normal, everything would be okay. I rubbed my cheek unconsciously. The blood…

"How much were you drinking the night I died? Think back now, clearly."

The night he died? I closed my eyes and shook my head. I didn't want to remember. Already the metallic tang of blood filled my nostrils, taking me back to that dark alley. The image of the trench coat woman's knife pressing down between Jo's lips before she…

I took a drag of the cigarette, filling my lungs and allowing it to wash over me. I calmed the beating of my heart and exhaled. When I opened my eyes, a hazy face appeared right before me, its mouth cut open from ear to ear in a horrific and mocking grin. It dissipated with the smoke. Laughter rang throughout the room as I jumped back.

"You will remember, Narumi. Don't worry about that."

I stood up and grabbed my wallet and keys. I didn't need anything else.

"We're not going to let you forget." Haruki this time. "You killed us, Narumi. You. How many more lives are you going to snuff out? How many more must die before you realise?"

I slammed the door behind me. Their laughter echoed inside the empty room of my apartment. I stubbed the cigarette out on the ground, rubbed my eyes, and pressed the button for the elevator. I couldn't be here anymore. Not alone, not like this. I had to be around people. Safety in numbers.

I had to go back to Rakucho.

23

RAKUCHO HAD CHANGED. DID THAT mean I had changed too? A can of beer in hand, I stumbled through the burgeoning crowds. I mean, it was in the name of the place; people came to Rakucho for fun. No serious business allowed. You left that at the giant gate signifying entry to another world. A world of pleasure. A world of hedonism. A world where all of your wildest desires could and would be satisfied.

Normally the throngs of bodies made me angry, but today they gave me relief. Even if the ghosts of the dead were whispering in my ear, I could not hear them. Not over the thrum of thousands of voices laughing, chatting, seducing, and selling. Young men in the latest fashion called to passersby from store entrances. They promised the attention of a bevy of beautiful babes, all ready and willing right now. Other men, more respectable in appearance, touted the latest and greatest award-winning food that you would only find in-store today. It didn't matter what they were selling. They all wanted your attention, and they would do whatever it took to get you inside. The feeling oddly warmed me. It was comfortable. Familiar.

It was home.

I passed by the sign at the end of the street, my own eyes—much younger and idyllic then—looking down at me. I couldn't meet their gaze. What a disappointment I'd turned into. If I had known that this was the future waiting for me, a washed up host with chronic smoker's cough, a dying liver, and more pains in my joints than a car crash victim, well…

I turned left, my feet carrying me on auto-pilot. A few streets away and they stopped of their own volition. Not that I minded. I had nowhere in particular to be.

My heart sank when I saw where I was. Sandy Shores. The first club I ever worked at. Or at least, it used to be Sandy Shores. Now women decorated the signage and advertised unbeatable rates on massage and other "services" designed to heal the body and mind. I didn't even know that Sandy Shores had closed down. I didn't earn a lot there, and I was never the most popular host—that honour belonged to Yuji, now long retired and ironically enough living out his life on some sandy beach somewhere—but it was my introduction to my calling. Sandy Shores taught me the ropes, and it was the place I learnt all the basic skills that I built upon to eventually become number one. Now it was a massage parlour for businessmen. It too was swallowed up with the passage of time. I set my jaw. I wouldn't be next. I made my own decisions about my future. Me. Nobody else.

A gang of yellows wandered by, four of them in total, laughing as one boy at the back thumbed through a wad of cash. One of them stopped as they were passing and sniffed the air. "You smell that?"

"Smell what?" his friend replied.

"Old man stench."

They burst out laughing and continued on their way. They had already disappeared around the corner by the time the can I threw after them hit the ground. They were long gone, and now I without a drink.

"Shitheads."

As much as I hated to admit it, something about them reminded me of my youth. Colour gangs were all the rage back then, and I nearly ended up in one myself. Again, ironically enough, it was Yotchan who stopped me. The same Yotchan who ended up joining the yakuza instead. Go big or go home was always how he lived his life, so that shouldn't have been a surprise, really.

Something wavered in the distance, just past the corner where the yellows disappeared. My heart jumped to my throat. That thing. Not Haruki, no, not him. He was just a voice in my head. A manifestation of my stress. Whatever that shaky, wobbly thing was, it was back. I prepared to run when a young woman emerged from the heat wave, numerous bags in either hand. I laughed and scratched the side of my head. A woman walking in the heat, nothing more.

A gang of blues were hot on her tail, however. Her eyes remained straight ahead, purposely ignoring their cat calls. She couldn't have been much older than 20, but she nervously glanced over at me as she walked past. I took a step to the side and in front of the blues as she continued on her way. It wouldn't be much, but it would be enough to let her disappear into the crowd while I distracted them.

"Boys, I was wondering if I could ask you a question."

"We're busy, grandpa."

"Hey, did anyone ever tell you that skinny jeans went out of fashion last decade?" another boy chimed in.

"Did anyone tell you that colours went out of fashion last generation?" I said. He narrowed his eyes. "No, seriously. I mean, if I'm a 'grandpa' as you claim, then that means the last time colours were in was when I, a grandpa, was a child. Surely if I'm a grandpa, again, as you claim, then that means you're following fashion from an entire generation ago. I'd like to think I know a little about fashion to begin with, but even to me that's kinda lame, don't you think?"

It was the alcohol talking. All the words I could never say while sober. The rational part of my brain would never let me. The drunk part though? Well, the unrestricted part of my brain was what got me to number one host and living one of the most lavish lifestyles in all of Rakucho. It couldn't have been that bad.

A punch swung for my face and I stepped back.

Stumbled back, really, but the end result was the same. He missed. A large group of businessmen walked by and the kids eyed them. One of the men pulled out his phone and looked directly at them as he spoke.

"Whatever, man. Let's get out of here." The head kid bumped into my shoulder as he passed by, his friends making sure to give me a pointed glance as if to say, "We won't forget this." The group of businessmen continued on. The man was on the phone with a client. He bowed his head slightly at me and continued on. My heart swelled. Rakucho looked out for its own. Even as a kid I knew that. Rakucho was a city of strangers, almost a country unto itself, smack bang in the middle of the capital, but people stuck together. We were all here for the same reason; fun. These colour gangs, though, they were like fleas on a dog's back. No-one wanted them and they brought nothing to the place other than annoyance. Nor, did it seem, that anyone could get rid of them. Decades after their heyday it appeared they were back again, and in stronger numbers than ever.

If they could come full circle, then I could too. I smiled. My feet carried me towards the closest convenience store. Grab a few beers, wait for nightfall, head over to the loudest club and enjoy some peace and serenity. It was a plan. I'd be seeing the surgeon at Smiling Bright the next day too. Just one more night to get through and then all my troubles would be over.

Yes. It was perfect. All was coming back around. Rakucho always provided. She was there for me when my own family wasn't. She took me from the gutter and raised me to the top. No-one was ever kinder to me than Rakucho was, and after a brief period of character building, she was giving back to me again. I didn't betray her. I never abandoned her like the others. They all wanted to turn tail at the slightest hint of disturbance. Betray the mother that had nurtured and raised them. Well, not me.

A dead voice called out "Welcome to Family Cart" as I stepped inside the building. Cool, crisp air-conditioning hit me in the face, a welcome respite from the oozing heat outside. I caught a brief glimpse of myself in the corner mirror sitting above the register. I smiled.

Soon. Soon I would take back what was mine.

24

A GRINNING FACE BEHIND A surgical mask greeted me. I attempted the best smile I could, but now that I was here, I was anything but relaxed.

"And how are you today, Mr Shinji?"

Mr Shinji. Nobody called me by that name. Even the boss called me Narumi. He'd known me since I was a kid, everyone had, so even now they called me Narumi. Mr Shinji made me sound old. I didn't like it.

"I'm fine, thanks. And call me Narumi."

"Of course, sir." He grinned again. My heart beat wildly in my chest. A tray of scalpels and other surgical tools sat on the trolley behind him. The lights overhead were so bright that I could barely see, and I wondered how he could. "I'm very glad you agreed to come see me again."

"Y-Yeah," I said. I had no second thoughts, but I did have raging fear. Scalpels. Why did it have to be scalpels? Several needles the length of my outstretched hand lay next to them and I shivered. Needles were even worse. I was the kid who tried to flee when it was needle time and had to be dragged kicking and screaming back to the doctor. When Yotchan showed me the massive tattoo covering his entire back, chest, and arms, I both marvelled and cringed. How he was able to withstand so many needles for such a long period of time, I'd never know. That made him the real hero. Needles made me go white and pass out. The doctor's gaze followed my own.

"Don't like needles?"

I nodded. He smiled. It was meant to be a reassuring gesture, but it was anything but.

"Don't worry, we're not going to be doing any cutting today."

I forced a smile and nodded, but in my nervousness, that still didn't make me feel any better. They were right there. What if he drugged me and then cut up my face? What if he did something to me while I was asleep? Was I even going to be drugged in the first place? He never explained anything about what was going to happen, and I never asked. He was a doctor. What was the worst he could do?

"Uh, what will we be doing today?"

He stood up and grabbed a file from his desk. "I'm glad you asked!" He sat down beside the chair I was on and opened to a few pages in. There were more diagrams of faces and a bunch of technical terms I'd never seen before. "Today we're going to be attempting a very simple procedure. It's in the final stages of testing, so I can guarantee you that this has already been performed on several people, and all with amazing results."

"Okay..."

"One of the biggest complaints we get, especially from men your age, is of wrinkles around the eyes and mouth."

I nodded.

"Until now, most customers have sought certain treatments to rectify that, but these treatments are..." he paused before continuing "...not the best."

"Not the best?"

He closed the file and shook his head. "More often than not, they come out looking unnatural. I'm sure you've seen it before. The human face ends up resembling somewhat of a wax doll, and the problem is that the procedure must be endured indefinitely. Once it stops, the wrinkles return."

"Oh." I didn't know what he was talking about, not exactly, but he was the doctor. He knew more than I did on the subject.

"This procedure, on the other hand, is a onetime deal. No cutting or surgery involved. There is a *little* injection involved, but that's all." He held his fingers up as he emphasised "little" and spoke as though he were speaking to a child. I tensed, and he patted me on the shoulder. "Just a little injection, of course. One here," he pressed next to my right eye, "one here," he pressed next to my left eye, "and then here and here." He pressed either side of my mouth as though his finger were the needle. I closed my eyes and nodded, not trusting my voice to speak the words I so desperately wanted to scream. *No needles!*

"Needles scare you that much, huh?"

"Is it that obvious?"

He grinned. "Your eyes have been flitting over to the table this whole time."

"Sorry…"

"Don't be. There's nothing to be afraid of. In fact, now you might laugh at this, but I have a fear of needles myself."

I raised my eyebrows. "But, you're a doctor."

"I am. It doesn't mean I'm immune to otherwise irrational fears like the rest of the world."

Irrational fears. There was nothing irrational about something long, sharp, and metal being jabbed into your skin and sliding through your flesh and all your pain receptacles. Nothing irrational at all.

"The good news," the doctor continued, "is that, for you at least, there are options."

I tilted my head. "What do you mean?"

He stood up and walked towards something in the corner of the room. "For procedures as delicate as this, we obviously don't want you moving around too much. We have done this numerous times before, both here and at associated facilities. We've never once had anything go wrong." He kept saying that. Nothing had ever gone wrong. It was having the opposite effect and making me more nervous than less. "But at the same time, we can't have our patients moving around during the procedure. One small mistake and it could cause some actual physical damage to the patient's face, and that is absolutely the last thing we want."

"Yes…" My voice trailed off. If this was his idea of a pep talk, it was failing greatly. He turned around and held a mask up. It looked like the ones I'd seen on TV before, the ones they used to put people to sleep. "W-What's that?"

"Sleeping gas. Just enough to make sure you're undisturbed during the procedure. You won't feel a thing, and for you, it'll be like you closed your eyes and then woke up a new man."

"A-Are you sure that's necessary?"

The doctor moved over to the table and held up a needle. "Well, which would you prefer?"

"The gas." My reply was instant. He smiled.

"Yes, I suspected as much. You don't have to worry—"

"—You've done this many times before, yes, I know." He was beginning to irritate me, but mostly my nerves were frayed. I wanted it over and done with. Give me back my youthful face. Let me go back to the life I once enjoyed so much.

The doctor pressed a button on the wall and a nurse came in. Her face was also covered by a mask. Everyone was covered but me, sitting there on the chair feeling naked to the world.

"Nurse, our patient has a fear of needles."

She nodded her head as though that perfectly explained everything and wheeled the gas over. "I-Is that legal?" I asked before I could stop myself. Was that how they did it? Gas tanks sitting on wheels. That didn't seem right. Before I could say anything else, the nurse was placing the mask over my nose and mouth. "No, wait, I—"

"Just count back from 10 with me. 10… 9…"

Her eyes glinted above me. Her smile grew beneath her mask, but something wasn't right about it. It was… too big. Too big? My heart pounded like a beating drum. This was wrong. Every nerve in my body screamed, my instincts going wild. They were knocking me out. They could do anything to me once I was gone. How well did I really know this doctor? It was too suspicious. Why didn't I question anything before I agreed to this?

"5… 4…"

I panicked, but the darkness was already settling in. Her smile grew even wider, like her jaw was about to unhinge and swallow me whole. It was the last thing I saw as my vision faded and the world went black.

"How are you feeling?"

Everything was dark. Sounds swarmed around me. My head swam. I blinked a few times, tiny spots of colour blinking in and out, slowly forming images, and then a face finally appeared above me.

"Ah!" I screamed. The nurse. Her unnaturally large mouth! She was going to eat me!

"Good to see your vocal cords still work," the doctor said, taking a step back. The skin on my face felt tight, like it was being pulled back by factory-strength staples, or I was standing head-on in gale force winds. I opened my mouth a few times, testing whether it could move against such tightness.

"What is…" I sounded like someone slugged me in the jaw and dislocated it. I could barely move.

"Stop fighting it. You just woke up, you need some time to get your bearings."

I put a hand up to my cheek and pulled it away. No blood. No cuts. My lips and cheeks were as they had always been. They didn't make me like that nurse. I melted back into the chair and breathed a sigh of relief.

"Expecting something else?" The doctor's eyes smiled. I tried to shake my head, but at best it lolled slightly. He patted me on the shoulder and pulled a chair closer to sit down. "The procedure was a raging success. I understand you're still feeling a little woozy right now, and that's natural." He leaned over and produced a mirror from the table behind him. He held it above me. "See?"

I reached up and touched my own face again. "Holy…"

"Right?" He grinned.

It was like looking at a version of myself from 20 years ago. The wrinkles around my eyes were all gone. The laugh lines completely disappeared. My cheeks glowed and the overall quality of my skin was nothing like when I got there. All I could do was laugh. The action felt strange and foreign, like I was baring my teeth from the tightness of my face, but inside I was joyous.

"Your face probably feels a little strange right now. A little tight and perhaps not quite your own. That's perfectly normal. It'll take a day or two for that feeling to go down, so don't worry. After that, you won't notice anything at all. Well, you might notice all the women fighting for your attention, but I imagine in your line of work that's probably not a bad thing, hey?"

Again I tried to smile. Again I bared my teeth like a wolf pretending it was human. He put the mirror down and stood up. "And if you're happy with everything, you can then proceed with the next step!"

"Next... step?" My voice floated away on the wind.

"Yes. This is just the first step. You are under no obligation to return, of course, but there's still so much more we can do for you yet."

So much more. What did that mean?

When I left the building 20 minutes later, his words continued to weigh on my mind. But more than that, as I stopped to look in the window reflection once more, they really had done an amazing job. They turned back the clock. I staggered towards the waiting taxi.

"Where to, sir?"

"Home." I gave the man the address and sank into the chair. For the first time since all this began, I felt like everything was going to be alright.

25

BY THE TIME I WOKE up, several days had passed. I checked my phone to make sure it wasn't bugging out and then turned the TV on. It wasn't lying. Two days had passed since I visited the doctor at Smiling Bright. Two entire days that I had no memory of.

"What the hell?"

My stomach growled like I had never eaten before. It certainly felt that way. An empty fridge greeted me as I opened the door. "Wonderful..." I lit a cigarette and sat back down on the couch, waiting for the fog to lift from my head. I touched my face and almost recoiled. It was so soft and smooth. I rubbed the area beside my eyes, what the women in the club sometimes called "crow's feet." Nothing. All smooth. I coughed a few times and waited for the pounding in my head to calm down. Well, my lungs were still old, but it was hard to argue with the doctor's results. There was very little swelling in my face, and despite the slight grogginess from too much sleep, I felt great!

I flicked through the channels on TV. Several messages from Koji were waiting for me on my phone, wondering how I was doing. I'd get back to him later. At the very least, that meant he was okay as well. Not that I thought he had much to worry about; he wasn't a host, after all. He just worked behind the bar.

Two days. I did a lot of shit in my youth, but I'd never slept through two straight days before. That sleeping gas was some good stuff. I smiled despite myself. It worked. It actually worked! I didn't even have to pay for it! My youthful looks were back, and unlike all those new punks coming in, I had the experience to back it up. That just left the problem of the club being closed...

"Another body was discovered in Rakucho in the early hours of the morning..." The announcer on TV drew my attention back. I sat up, eyes wide. Not again... "Police have yet to reveal any concrete details, but witnesses claim that the victim was yet another host from Rakucho's bustling entertainment district..." There it was. Another host. Another host had been killed while I was asleep. As much as I hated to admit it, a small part of me was relieved. If that trench coat woman really was trying to frame me, then she fucked up. I was asleep at home the entire time. There was no blood in my apartment, no blood on my clothes, nothing. I was asleep. Right here. No witnesses. No way to link me to it.

She fucked up.

My stomach growled, louder this time. I put the cigarette out and grabbed my keys and wallet. A little breakfast in Rakucho to calm the stomach, and a little surveillance of the area for information. I needed to know who it was. At this point, there was no way the police weren't going to shut all the clubs down. Everyone would be out of work, and only the most industrious folks would find a way to flip it to their advantage. Folks like me.

I strode through the main street, chest high and grin wide. I was a new man and everyone deserved to know it. The street was as busy as ever, almost as if no-one cared that several murders had taken place over the last week or so. Probably no-one did. That was also the sad reality of Rakucho, but one I had embraced long ago. Many passed through Rakucho looking for a quick bit of fun and not looking to engage with anyone. Those were not the people who called Rakucho home. Those were the fleas on the dog's back. Necessary to Rakucho's economy, sure, but they didn't look out for her and she didn't look out for them. Rakucho was a small bump in their day (or night) and nothing more. She wasn't home to them like she was to me. 'Well, mother, I'm back.'

Club Tenshi's doors remained closed. Nothing had changed. I wasn't expecting much different, but the stark reality before me was still upsetting. I honestly felt better than ever. Not just my face, which felt rejuvenated, but my energy levels, and my confidence levels. The pain in my shoulder was still there, yes, as was the odd throbbing in my knee, and nothing could be done about that cough now, but setting all those things aside... I was ready and raring to go. How could I do that if everything was closed?

"Hurry up, man, come on!" A voice, frantic and whispered, found its way to me around the corner. It was coming from behind the club. I stuck my head around the wall; a group of greens had a screwdriver jammed into the door, trying to jiggle it open. "I thought you said you knew how to do this?"

"Shut it! There's no need to rush, so stop wetting your panties. They've been closed for days now, and nobody comes out this way when the sun's up anyway, so shut it!"

I stepped forward and made myself known. "Boys." They jumped back and tried to hide the screwdriver, watching helplessly as it fell to the ground and rolled towards my feet. "Something I can help you with?"

The kid who had been jiggling the screwdriver pulled out a pocket knife. He thrust it in my direction. "You didn't see anything, now get outta here!" His voice wavered, as did his hand, but he held his ground.

"Oh, but I did. I saw you trying to break into my club." The kid swallowed at that, but he refused to back down.

"Shit, man, he works here!"

"He's seen our faces!"

"So what?" the kid with the knife screamed. He lowered it slightly and straightened his back, attempting to make himself look taller. If it was his attempt at being intimidating, it wasn't very successful. He was still smaller than me. "We're not the ones who should be worried here."

I raised an eyebrow. The sensation was strange and off-putting. Like my eyebrow was no longer my own. It wasn't something that happened naturally, but like I gave an internal command and then it followed. Odd. The tightness in my face was also unrelenting, but it would take some time to wear off. Nothing to be concerned about. "If you're suggesting that I need to be afraid of that little pin-prick you have there, then you boys clearly haven't been around Rakucho for very long."

"This?" The boy laughed. "No, not this. *Her*."

My heart skipped a beat. They knew about her? The trench coat woman? The boy's lopsided grin grew larger. He continued to hold the knife before him, but the nerves in his body seemed to melt away and he grew less tense. "Yeah, you know who I'm talking about, don't you?"

I took a step forward without thinking. He raised his knife suddenly, and I held my hands up. "What do you know about her? Tell me!"

The boy side-eyed his buddy and shrugged. "I know she's been good for business. Ever since she appeared, all your clubs have been closing and leaving their shit inside. Good shit, you know? Good for business. *Our* business."

I didn't care about that. "No, what do you know about *her*? Who is she? Why is she doing this?" The who part was less pertinent; I already knew that. Mostly. Kinda. Somewhat. I didn't know her name or anything about her, really. Koji said the woman in the mask, the woman I saw in the club with Haruki before she disappeared upstairs and put on her trench coat, was a former customer of mine, but for the life of me I couldn't remember her. Her name started with Mi... something. Names were never my forte. We didn't keep records of customers, and she had no tab, so we had no idea who she really was, nor where to find her. But her reasons for being here now, for killing hosts, that I very much wanted to know.

Again the boy shrugged. "Her beef is with you guys, not us."

"So you *have* seen her?"

"Of course," the boy behind the leader chimed in. "I ran into her two nights ago."

I brushed past the boy with the knife and grabbed his friend. "What is she doing here? Tell me what you know!"

He looked at me for a moment before smiling. "Hey, I know you. We ran into you a few days ago. You looked a lot rougher then, shit. Not that I blame you, what with all the hosts getting murdered and shit."

As much as I hated it, my heart jumped. It worked. I didn't remember who this kid was, but considering the amount of colour gangs in Rakucho lately, that didn't especially faze me. But he knew who I was, and he recognised that I looked better. The doctor did it. He really did it. I shook my head to clear the thoughts. The pounding in the base of my skull and temples was returning, but serious business first. "Why is she killing us? What does she want?"

"Beats me, man. But hey, why don't you go run along now and leave us to our business. You're lucky you didn't get roughed up last time, but I don't think we'll be so generous this time, yeah?" He patted me on the cheek a few times, even as I was holding onto the front of his green sweater. It felt like 40 degrees already and sweat pooled beneath me, and these kids were wearing long green pants and sweaters. Kids these days…

"Generous, huh?"

His friend with the knife placed his arm across mine. He didn't force me to let go, but placed enough pressure to let me know his intent. Let go, or we'll be forced to make you. He positioned his knife by my stomach. "Yeah, generous."

I kicked the kid in knee and he dropped with a sickening crunch, his knife clattering to the ground. I pulled the kid I was already holding closer and my fist connected with his temple. He crumpled to the ground like a sack of rocks. Adrenaline coursed through me. Everything came flooding back in an instant. It was just like my teenage years running the streets with Yotchan, before either of us knew what we were going to do with the rest of our lives and had no care for what happened, anyway. We took what Rakucho provided, and we learnt to live within her walls by any means possible.

Another boy jumped over his groaning friend and threw himself at me. We stumbled back a few steps and I grabbed his arm, twisting it up behind his back. I pushed him over towards the garbage and slammed his face into the large, hot metal container. He screamed and fell to his knees, blood dripping on the ground. I imagined I could almost hear it sizzle.

Why had I ever found these kids to be a threat?

CHAPTER TWENTY-FIVE

They crumpled at the first sign of challenge.

"Hey, I got another question for you." I yanked the kid back up and squeezed my forearm tight around his neck. He looked at his friends, pleading as he choked against the pressure, but they remained frozen on the spot. "If you know about the trench coat woman, then maybe you've seen the..." The what? I didn't know what it was, or even if it was real. The wavy, wobbly thing. I'd been under a lot of stress, and as the kids in their stupid green clothes stared back at me, trembling and wide-eyed, I sighed and threw the boy back at them. "You know what, never mind. Just my mind playing tricks on me, I guess."

Confusion painted their features. Good. The boy on the ground reached out for his knife. I stood on his hand and pushed down with my boot. He squealed.

"You sure you don't know anything about that woman?" He shook his head. Tears ran down his cheeks. I clucked. "Huh. Too bad." I removed my boot from his hand and squatted before him. I picked his knife up and handed it back. "Listen, this here is my place of work. I know you boys remember me." I stopped and looked at each of them pointedly. "And I remember you. If I ever see you again, or if anything happens to my club before we reopen, I'm going to find you, you hear me? I've been in Rakucho since before you little shits were even born. I will find you, and next time, it won't be so pretty. Got it?"

The boy nodded. I slapped his cheek a few times and stood up.

"Now, get out of my sight."
Shinji Narumi was back. With a vengeance.

26

I WAS ON TOP OF the world. I showed those punks who was boss. They even remarked on how much younger I looked. It worked. It actually worked. I'd have to give the doc a call and let him know, and perhaps schedule a few later appointments while I was at it. Of course, it had only been a few days—if the clock was anything to go by—but if this was the kind of work he could do with a simple... whatever he did... then who was I to argue? It wouldn't be long until the money was rolling in, and paying for a few more tiny procedures here and there would be nothing. You gotta invest in your business if you want it to make money. *I* was that business. If I didn't look good, why would the customers want to spend their money on me? Simple business sense.

Strolling down the street, I took everything in. Heat wavered in the distance, no matter what direction I looked. Usually it got me down, but not today. Today it was a welcome blanket, and almost took me back to my early childhood. The few memories I had of my family, together and happy. Playing at the beach. Going to the local summer festival. I wouldn't say they were better times, but easier, for sure. Until…

I shook my head. Flowers bloomed in the small area just off the main street that was designated as a park. As night fell, it filled with drunks and people taking shortcuts, but in the daylight it was full of colour and beauty. A bright spot in what was otherwise considered the "immoral capital of the East." She was Rakucho's oft-ignored beauty. Not big enough to make an impact, but small enough to remain significant amongst otherwise the drab buildings. I picked a flower and sniffed it. I could allow myself a few moments to be corny.

Something buzzed near my ear. I swiped at it, thinking it a bee, but I soon realised it wasn't near my ear, it was *inside* my ear. Inside my head, to be exact. My head was buzzing. It wasn't the usual low buzz I always heard, nor was it what I felt during my frequent migraines. I shook my head. No pain, just a buzz. I made my way past the giant sign advertising, well, me, and took a right. Further into Rakucho. I stuck my finger in my ear and wiggled, but nothing. The buzz continued. I tried both ears. The buzz intensified.

"What the hell?"

A gang of yellows were sizing up a smaller gang of blues at the end of the street. I walked past them and they took no notice of me. Several people moved to the other side of the street to avoid them, eyes down and feet picking up the pace. Someone really ought to do something about them, I thought. I could stop and try to take on the 10 or so teens that were there, about to make a fuss that would no doubt bring the police running, but what good would that do anyone? Not like they'd have a change of heart and leave Rakucho forever. Even if I did rough them all up enough to stop a fight, there was no telling that one of them wouldn't get a lucky hit in and mess my face—my business—up. Nor that the police wouldn't arrest *me* for beating on some kids.

Not today. I'd already done my part. I ignored them and continued on.

The buzz grew louder. I crouched over, head in my hands. It was the strangest sensation. Not quite a headache, not quite tinnitus, but something else. Like a bee inside my brain. Buzz buzz. Let me out. A convenience store was just ahead. The doorbell tinkled.

"Welcome to Family Cart." A young woman greeted me, her tone far more alive than the usual cashier. I grinned and grabbed a basket. She was cute. I filled it with aspirin, a rice ball, and a six pack of *shochu*.

"Aren't you scared?"

"Huh?"

Her voice drew me from my thoughts as she scanned the items. She gave me the once over while she continued scanning and placing the items in a bag.

"Aren't you scared? You know, of the host killer?"

The host killer. So that's what they called her

around here. It made sense. She had only killed hosts, after all. Although, it lacked the same punch as the Rakucho Nightcrawler.

"Why should I be?" I replied.

"Well, this person's killed three or four people already. All hosts. I don't mean to pry, what you do is your own business, but dressing like that probably isn't the safest right now…"

She said it like my job was something to be ashamed off. Something dirty. My grin grew even larger.

"I'm not afraid of anything," I said. "In fact, I think from here on out, things are going to get a lot better."

The cashier raised her eyebrow but said nothing. She handed me the bag, and I pushed the notes across the table. I didn't have many left, but that shouldn't be a problem for much longer. Shinji Narumi, the number one host of Rakucho, was back in business and ready to slay the ladies. Not literally, of course. Just their wallets and perhaps their emotions. I couldn't help it if they fell in love with me. It wouldn't be the first time that ever happened. But first, I had to find that woman. Mitsuko. Mitsumi. Minami. Whatever her name was. It was like the surgery gave me new life, new confidence. I could do anything. She didn't scare me. Nothing scared me! Other than, perhaps, keeping Club Tenshi closed and letting this handsome face go to waste. No, I would find that trench coat woman, and I would stop her. This couldn't continue any longer. Whatever her point was, she'd made it. Now it was time to stop.

The buzz in my head grew louder. It was almost imperceptible, but the more I focused on it, the more I realised it was getting both louder and more persistent.

"What time do you finish work today?" I asked the young woman before me. She raised her eyebrows for a moment before laughing and then shaking her head.

"Oh, sorry. Um, I'm working late tonight. Double shift."

"Excellent. I am a creature of the night, after all." It sounded better in my head, but I rolled with it. She, however, was less than impressed.

"No offence, but I don't feel especially safe going out with someone of your... occupation."

I smiled. My occupation. There it was again, like it was a dirty word. Here, in Rakucho, of all places. "Well, if you ever change your mind, just check the giant billboard at the end of main street. You'll find me there."

She slowly nodded, and I took the bag with a wink. Stepping back out into the heat, I grabbed a can and downed it like I had finally found my oasis in the desert. I walked through the empty streets of Rakucho, finding myself drawn deeper into her belly, emptying cans as I went. How long passed? An hour? Two hours? 20 minutes? It didn't matter. I realised, however, that the longer I walked and the more I drank, the less I noticed that awful buzz in my head. I felt exactly like I had when I was 20. Energy flowed through me, revitalising me.

As a teen I was unstoppable, or so I thought, and that carried through most of my 20s. Few hosts or clients could keep up with my alcohol consumption and partying. If you needed a man to down a drink, Shinji Narumi was that man. It was a neat trick at first. One of the older hosts I looked up to when I first started, Yuji, called me over one night and handed me an unopened bottle of champagne. It didn't take a genius to see that it was our most expensive brand, the type that sold for more than I made in several months' salary. "Drink it," he said. "Drink the entire bottle in one go, and if you can, I'll let you drink with us for the rest of the night." It was an offer I couldn't refuse. If you were the new kid, you didn't turn down an offer from the big guy himself to join his posse. Little did he know that I was a master and barely a dribble escaped my lips as I chugged the entire thing. His client whooped and cheered and several days later she returned; not for him, but for me. That was the start of my career. All because of a single bottle of champagne.

"And they tell me to stop drinking you," I said to the empty can in my hand, tossing it into a nearby bin. I was that young man again, full of life, full of vigour, full of desire to be the best and possessing the skills to make that happen. Only now, I was even better. I had decades of experience behind me. I knew exactly what it was like to be number one, and I would do whatever it took to get back there again.

But first, I had to find that woman.

27

BY THE TIME NIGHT FELL, I was no better off than I was that morning. I was more drunk, for sure, but no better off on the trench coat woman front. Or the nightcrawler. Or the host killer. Whatever they called her. Not that I really expected to find her wandering around the streets of Rakucho in broad daylight, but what else could I do?

The alcohol kept the buzz at bay. I didn't know why and I didn't care, either. Drunk was a state I knew well and, if I was perfectly honest, the state I was most comfortable in. I wasn't going to argue with results, not when it was something I didn't mind to begin with.

I called Koji. He was watching TV at home, and after screaming at me for several minutes about how much of an asshole I was for disappearing, he finally calmed down enough for me to talk to him.

"Koji, listen, I need you to tell me about that woman again."

"What woman?" he said.

"The one from the club last week. With the mask. Remember?"

He was silent a few moments before answering. "Mizuki?"

"Yes! That's her! I knew there was a 'mi' in her name somewhere!"

"…What do you want to know about her?"

"Everything."

Silence. "…Are you sure you're okay, Narumi? You sound a little… Do you need me to come out there and pick you up? With everything that's going on, I don't think you should be—"

"What? No!" He thought I was drunk and raving. "I just need you to tell me everything about that woman!"

"I don't know anything about her. You know we don't keep that kind of information. If anyone would know anything about her, it would be you. She was your customer." Shit. "I can come out and get you, Narumi. Then we can—"

"Look, thanks Koji. Sorry. I gotta go." I hung up before he could attempt to talk me out of what I knew I needed to do. Mizuki. Mizuki was my client. I knew she was the trench coat woman. I knew it. I saw her. She had a mask when she came to the club. She put on a large coat when she left. She grinned at me. I couldn't see it behind the mask, sure, but I saw her eyes. They were grinning. She wanted me to know. The only question was, why?

I sat down on a small hill by the street and threw my empty can to the ground.

"Hey, buddy. Not sure if you have a great sense

of humour or a great sense of irony."

My heart fell.

"What, didn't think you'd be rid of me that easily?"

"Go away." I was speaking to myself, I knew it, but I was not in the mood to deal with him.

"Do you even realise where you're sitting? That's a bit rude."

I looked over at the grass and a dark sensation washed over me.

"Atta boy. You know, I think you picked this spot on purpose. Criminals always return to the scene of their crime at some point, you know."

It was where I saw her that time. Where I saw her nearly cutting Jo's head in two. A voice whispered by my right ear.

"You won't get away with it that easily..."

I waved the voice away, like trying to shoo a fly. It giggled, this time by my left ear.

"I didn't do anything!"

"Keep telling yourself that."

I closed my eyes and opened my last can. I just wanted the voices to be quiet. I wanted the buzz to be quiet. Why couldn't everything just be quiet?!

"How are you enjoying your new face?" Another voice again. Haruki. I shuddered. He was the last person I wanted to hear from about my looks.

"It's not a new face."

"Sure. You just visited the plastic surgeon and all of a sudden you're 20 years younger. Naturally, of course."

"It's not new." I swiped by my left ear. "I just had some help. Everyone has something done eventually, why should I be different?"

"Is that what this is? You're honestly trying to claim that you're just being like everyone else? You?"

"Go away." Shochu dribbled down my chin. I let it. The tightness was still there, but what did they know? It wasn't like I transferred a new face onto my own, or even changed my own face. I was still the same old Narumi, just with fewer wrinkles. Honestly, what was wrong with that? I was investing in my business. What right did Haruki of all people have to look down upon that?

"'Go away.' I think he's upset."

"Aww, poor baby. It must all finally be getting to him."

The voices circled around my head. I feared that if I opened my eyes, I would see them both standing there before me, their faces bloody and eyes full of judgement. Or worse, one of them would be holding the trench coat woman's knife, ready to drag me down with them. I took another drink. The buzz in the back of my brain was dying down, but in return, *they* were getting louder. So this was it, huh? One or the other. The frying pan or the fire.

"Where is she?" I asked. The voices stopped for a moment, and then Haruki answered by my right ear.

"Who?"

"The woman. You know who." They said nothing. For the first time, both of them fell silent. "I intend to stop her from harming anyone else. But first, I need to know where she is." I opened my eyes and was greeted with several businessmen making their way past me, moving to the other side of the street as they did so. Yeah, laugh it up, boys. Just another crazy man getting drunk in the gutter. Go on, keep walking. Faster now. "Come on. You're ghosts, aren't you? Why else would you keep bothering me? Well, if you're going to continue making my life a living hell, the least you can do is tell me where she is so I can stop this from happening to another person."

"…He doesn't get it, does he?"

"…No, it would appear that he doesn't."

"Get what?" They were pissing me off. I wasn't sure what was worse; actually seeing them there before me, blood and all, or just being assaulted by their bodiless voices. At least the bloody faces gave me something to visualise. This just made me seasick.

"The poor thing."

"He'll find out soon enough, right?"

"I would say so. Not much longer now."

I stood up and threw my can across the street in a rage. "Find out what?" Some school girls hurried by, dodging the liquid as the can smashed into the hard pavement.

"It's you, Narumi."

I spun around, but I still couldn't see them. "What's me? Show yourselves!" I turned and found myself face-to-face with Jo, the man who died on the very same spot I was standing on. I jumped back in fright and then clenched my fists. "What's me?" I repeated, calmer this time. He turned to his left and seemed to cringe at something only he could see. He vanished before my eyes, leaving only a few scared words in his wake.

"It's you she wants, Narumi. It's you."

28

IT WAS ME? WHAT DID that even mean? But the voice was gone, and for the briefest of moments a now-unfamiliar sensation washed over me; peace. It was soon replaced by fear, and a dark, creeping dread began to settle in. It was me. What was me? Why did she want me? Why was she killing other hosts and not me if it was me that she wanted? Nothing made sense. For the last few weeks now, nothing had made any sense. The world was falling apart around me and I was watching it happen.

I turned in the direction Jo look before his ghostly face contorted with fear and disappeared. It was her. It had to be. He was afraid of her, and that was why he haunted me. If he was real at all and not just a product of my imagination. But supposing for a moment that he was real, Jo knew me. I was at the scene of the crime when the trench coat woman brutally murdered and disfigured him. Even in death, he was afraid of her. He took that anger out on me. A flame sparked in my chest and I strode down the street. People jumped out of my way. The sun was gone, and this was the Rakucho I was most familiar with. Most comfortable in. This was my mother, and I knew my way around her better than I knew the back of my own hand. Which, when you thought about it, was an odd saying. Who spent that much time looking at the back of their hand? I wouldn't be able to tell mine from the next guy's.

Before long, I realised I had no idea where I was going, but the alcohol swimming through my system propelled me forward, and I was not going to argue with it. The confident strides I saw myself taking no doubt existed only in my mind, and a brief glimpse of myself in the mirror showed that I was perhaps not as tall and strong as I thought myself to be. A little stagger in my step did nothing to diminish my purpose. The side eyes and glances of people walking by meant nothing to me. Rakucho taught you to develop a thick skin, and mine was made of steel. Harden up or get buried in her seedy depths. Learn to swim, or quickly drown. That wasn't me. That was never me.

My feet carried me deeper into Rakucho's belly. The main street serviced the majority of the public and was filled to the brim with restaurants, arcades, and some of the "safer" entertainment options. But the further in you went, the more "anything goes" Rakucho became. Some of my best memories were deep in the underbelly of Rakucho, in the areas even the police were hesitant to enter. They preferred to let folks sort their own beefs out, and only showed up when absolutely necessary. If a body showed up this far from Rakucho's safe, public face, you could bet that someone would clean it up before the police got word of it, and even if they did, they would take their time before coming out to investigate. Enough time to make sure that body disappeared first.

The lights were fewer out here. Darker. I passed a gang of purples sitting on their haunches under one of the lights. They watched me stagger by and one boy stood up. His friend grabbed his sleeve and shook his head. He sat back down and several sets of eyes watched me go. The further I walked, the fewer people I saw. After everything that had happened over the last few weeks, the silence was deafening. No buzz. No voices. Nothing but the vague throbbing of an impending hangover and the strange tightness in my face.

She was out here. No doubt about it. Something was taking me to her. It was me. She wanted me. Rakucho was taking me to her—for what reason, I didn't know—but finally I would put an end to all this. Stop her reign of terror. Get back to work. Get my life back in order. Only this time, I would be smarter. Treat my money better. Be more aware of the world around me. Take note of my customers' names and remember them this time. I had perhaps a few short years left in me before I really would have to retire, so I had to make the best of this opportunity. Save for the future. Get my life sorted out. Be the man I was always meant to be. Not just number one in name, but in spirit as well.

The only thing standing between me and my dream life was that woman.

I turned the corner and stopped dead in my

tracks. A hot, humid wind blew over me, caressing my face and ruffling my hair. I placed a hand on the wall to steady myself, my eyes unsure of what they were taking in. A choked sound escaped my parched throat, and I gaped like a fish out of water.

It was her. She was right there. Standing over the body of another young man. Blood splattered her white mask and dripped from the tip of her knife. The knife that was pressed into the man's throat.

"Why?" My voice came out as a harsh choke. "Why are you doing this?"

She smiled and pressed the knife tighter into the man's throat. Cuts marred his face and blood stained his clothes, but he was otherwise fine. Perhaps "fine" wasn't the best word to describe his situation. Alive. The man was still alive. I didn't have to ask him whether he was also a host. His clothes and hairstyle gave that away. I had no immediate knowledge of who the man was, but he looked familiar. A top host from a rival club, perhaps.

"Please!" He reached out towards me. "Help me!"

She jabbed the knife into his skin harder, a trickle of blood making its way down his neck and over his collarbone. His chest rose and fell rapidly, like he was hyperventilating. His hands trembled, but he didn't dare move. Not when she literally held his life in her hands.

I held a hand up before me and inched closer. "Whatever this is, I'm sure we can talk about it."

She leaned down over the man and, with her free hand, cupped his bloody cheek. She caressed it like a lover and then grabbed his hair and yanked his head back.

"No!"

The man whimpered, but she did not kill him. She kept her eyes focused on me. I looked up and down the street, but we were alone. Light from the streetlight several metres down the road cast a hazy glow over the area, but it was enough.

"It's me you want, right?" Maybe I could bargain with her. I wasn't sure how I was going to stop her exactly, but thinking ahead was never one of my strong points. First, I just had to get her away from that guy and then we'd go from there.

Yet she didn't answer. Instead, she slid the knife up the man's neck and pressed it into his cheek. Blood trickled down, and his choked screams drew louder as she pushed the knife in, cutting his cheek all the way down to the mouth. The knife scraped against his clenched teeth, a sound that gave me nightmares. His breathing became even more shallow and rapid. She wasn't killing him, she was mangling him. Torturing him. Pain tore up my own cheek in sympathy. She was removing the one thing that gave him an advantage in life: his good looks.

Tears spilt from his cheeks to the hot asphalt below. His eyes pleaded with me while he screamed through his clenched jaw.

"Just let him go. Take me instead." He was as good as done for now. He'd never work as a host again, not like that. But he could still get away with his life. At the very least, he could have that.

She pulled his head back and jammed the knife into his throat.

"No!"

Blood gushed forth as she carved his neck like it was a roast dinner, almost taking his head clean off. I ran forward, screaming. Tips of a horrific mouth peeked out from behind her mask, reaching all the way up to her ears as she laughed manically. She wasn't human. She was a monster. A real, live monster. All she had to do was open her head a little wider and she could devour him whole, and I would be next. Her mouth… H-Her teeth… She…

A rock in the middle of the road halted my progress. A tiny, simple rock. The road rushed up to meet me, and before I could ponder it any further, the world went black. In the distance, her high-pitched laugh continued, and then slowly faded away.

29

MY HEAD POUNDED LIKE A jackhammer was being driven into my ear. Something on my wrist rattled as I went to grab my head, and as my eyes slowly came back into focus, I was greeted by handcuffs. A shot of adrenaline coursed through me. I was handcuffed to a bed in a jail cell, a man in a suit standing over me.

"Told you he'd be fine," he said to someone on the other side of the bars. "He bumped his head, that's all. No doubt from all the alcohol he consumed."

My head swam. Where was I? Who was this man? What was going on?

"Who are—"

He knelt down and flashed a blinding light in my eyes. "Follow my finger." He moved a hand in front of my face, not that I could see it after he blinded me with his torch. After a few moments he stopped, stood up, and tapped on the bars. "He's fine. He'll have a hell of a hangover, no doubt, but no lasting damage."

The officer on the other side jangled his keys and a few moments later the man in the suit walked out. I attempted to get to my feet and was pulled back down on the bed again. The damn handcuffs.

"What is—"

"No talking," the officer replied. His words rattled like a hammer trying to find a hollow spot inside my head. I closed my eyes again and lay back. Jail. I was in jail. I'd never been to jail before, not even after all my antics as a kid. Yotchan. I had to get into contact with him. He'd know what to do. This was his world, not mine.

I waited for the pounding to come down to a tolerable level and then heard rattling at the door again. This time two officers entered, a male and a female, and the female unlocked the cuffs tying me to the bed.

"Follow us," the man said. His partner fastened the cuff around my other wrist and guided me out. I didn't know where I was, but it wasn't a large station. Just a few empty cells and a door on either side of the hall. I had to be near Rakucho.

Rakucho. The memories came flooding back. The woman in the trench coat, Mizuki. The host. The knife. The blood. The...

"Sit down." The male officer pushed me into a chair in a separate questioning room and moved to the other side of the table. His partner stood in the corner, writing something in her notes, while he paced before me.

"You know why you're here, right?"

I gulped. I could guess, but it wasn't me! I didn't kill the man! I looked down. My shirt and pants were covered in blood. His blood, no doubt. No matter how you looked at it, it didn't look good.

"I don't—"

"Don't lie to me!" The man slammed his fist down on the desk and I jumped. The pounding in my head raged, and I struggled to see him through blurry eyes. They refused to focus. They just wanted sleep.

"I'm not—"

"Where were you last night?" he continued. I glanced over at the woman in the corner, barely making out her vague silhouette. A single light flickered above, making it difficult to see her. I flinched, images of the trench coat woman—no, Mizuki—coming back to me. She wasn't the trench coat woman. Her name was Mizuki. Someone I knew. Or, someone I should have known. She knew me, but if I were to be entirely honest with myself, I had no memories of her. The officer in the corner glanced up from her file and I could have sworn she smiled at me. Her grin spreading up to her ears, her mouth so large, her teeth so sharp that she could lean forward and rip my entire head off. I closed my eyes and shook the images away.

"Rakucho," I said. "I was in Rakucho."

The male officer started pacing again. "And what were you doing in Rakucho?"

Drinking. Looking for a serial killer. Watching a man die. "Just walking around."

The officer nodded, as though that was the answer he was expecting and it made perfect sense.

"Just walking around. I see. Excuse me for being presumptuous, but you are a host, yes?"

I nodded.

"I'll need you to answer me out loud at all times."

"Yes," I replied.

"Okay. Where do you work? Which club?"

"Club Tenshi…"

"Club Tenshi." He turned and nodded to his partner. She pulled her phone out and whispered something to the person on the other end. "And were you working last night?"

I shook my head.

"Out loud, sir."

"No." His voice boomed like waves crashing against the rocks of my head. The light continued to flicker in and out, bringing with it an all too familiar buzz. Or maybe it wasn't the light…

"No? You weren't working, and yet you're dressed like…" He held his hands out before him. "If you weren't working, then what were you doing in Rakucho last night?"

"Like I told you, I was walking around."

He laughed. "You'll have to forgive me if I find that a little hard to believe. You can surely understand where I'm coming from." He planted his hands firm on the desk and looked closely at me. "Look, I'm going to get straight to the point. A man died in Rakucho last night. Murdered, to be more precise. You were discovered next to his body, knife in hand and covered in his blood. He's not the first host to die in Rakucho over the last week. Now, if we go and search your apartment right now, can you honestly tell me that we won't find anything connecting you to those murders as well?"

My heart threatened to burst out of my chest. My mouth was so dry that my tongue felt like sandpaper. I didn't trust myself to answer him out loud. Would they find anything there? I was careful not to leave anything incriminating around, wasn't I?

…The knife.

"I didn't do it…"

"I'm sorry, you'll have to speak a little louder."

Water. I needed water. "I didn't do it," I said a little louder. The officer turned to his partner and raised his eyebrows.

"Okay, I'll humour you. If you didn't do it, then who did?"

"T-The woman."

He tilted his head. "The woman?" He didn't believe a word I was saying. I couldn't blame him.

"Could I get a glass of water?" I asked. Again he turned and nodded to his partner and she knocked on the door. She whispered something to the man on the other side and he disappeared.

"What woman?"

"H-Her name is Mizuki." Death surely felt better than the agony in my head, the cotton in my mouth, and the overall pain and exhaustion flooding my body. I felt like I'd gone several rounds with a heavyweight and, unsurprisingly, didn't get a single hit in. The woman's pen moved furiously, and then there was a knock at the door again. A glass of water. Finally.

"Okay, who is this 'Mizuki'?" the officer asked

as I downed the glass in one go. Rivulets of water dribbled down my chin and I closed my eyes for a brief moment of bliss.

"She's uh, a customer of mine. I think."

The officers glanced at each other. "You think?"

I shrugged. "So I'm told."

The officer nodded and started pacing again. "So you're told... Okay, so, just to get things straight, we found you next to the body—with the murder weapon in hand—covered in the victim's blood, but it wasn't you. It was one of your customers. Maybe. A woman named Mizuki. Does Mizuki have a last name?"

I shrugged again. "I don't know."

"You don't know. A woman who may or may not be one of your customers, because I've no doubt you see so many that they really must be difficult to keep track of—" the woman laughed in the corner "—and all you know is that her name is Mizuki. I gotta level with you... What's his name again?" He turned to his partner.

"Shinji. Shinji Narumi," she said.

"Shinji Narumi. Of course. I knew a Narumi in elementary school. Everybody picked on him because he was so tiny. Anyway, Mr Shinji, you gotta see how this doesn't look good for you."

No, it didn't. But it was the truth.

"I can describe her!" I said. "She wears a trench coat and, uh, a face mask. A white face mask. She has long hair and..." the officers were staring at me "...What?"

"A face mask? Trench coat?"

"Yes."

CHAPTER TWENTY-NINE

"We're going to need a little more to go off than that."

"…That's what she wears."

The officer straightened up and sighed. "Why did you kill the man, Mr Shinji? Or should I call you Narumi?"

"Narumi is fine, and I didn't kill him."

He slammed the desk again. His partner didn't even flinch. She was no doubt used to this act. "Last chance, Narumi. This is only going to get worse for you, not better. If you work with us now, then we can make things easier for you down the line. It doesn't have to be the death penalty."

Death penalty? Whoa, nobody mentioned anything about the death penalty. "It wasn't me! I didn't do it! It was her! Mizuki! You have to find her before she kills someone else again! You're wasting your time! The next death will be on your hands, not mine!"

Blood pumped through my veins, pushing the boiling anger along until it overflowed. They weren't listening, and they had no intention of listening. They wanted me to confess so they could move on and wrap this case up, a quick win. Rakucho's host killer arrested and put to death. The capital is safe once again! Only it wasn't me. They had the wrong person, and by the time they realised that, it would be too late.

But how on earth was I going to convince them of that?

30

HOW MANY DAYS PASSED? WITH no window to the outside, it was impossible to tell. They were allowed to hold me for several weeks without charging me, or so they said, but they wanted me to confess. It would be easier for me that way, they said. Things would go a lot better and they could get the death penalty off the table if I just confessed to my crimes. That was all I needed to do. Confess. But there was one problem with that.

I didn't do it.

Life became an endless cycle of wake up, eat breakfast, do laundry, clean cell, undergo questioning, eat lunch, undergo more questioning, eat dinner, read books, and then bed. All accompanied by an annoying, sometimes almost deafening, buzz. Every day. It was the only way for me to tell that time was passing at all. I was used to life without sunlight; night was my domain ever since I was a teenager. This, though, this was something else.

They wouldn't allow me to call anyone. Not Yotchan, not Koji, not the boss; no-one. I wasn't allowed to do anything until I confessed. Day after day they presented me with the evidence and motives of my crimes. They had me, short of my confession. They would take me to court and they would get me convicted, regardless of whether I confessed, but it would be easier for all if I did. And better for me, because I might get out of it with my life. No matter how many times I told them "it wasn't me" it didn't seem to matter. Day by day they worked to break me, and they would no longer entertain my suggestions that it wasn't me but a woman. A woman in a trench coat and face mask. It sounded crazy, and it probably was, but that didn't change the fact that it was the truth.

I rested my forehead against the table as the usual duo of cops questioned me yet again. "I told you, it was the woman."

"The one in the trench coat and mask, yes, we know, you've told us several times. But the problem with that is that we don't believe you." This time the female officer took the lead, while her male partner stood in the back of the room. It was like he never blinked. He watched everything taking place before him and no doubt could recall it in excruciating detail if necessary.

"I don't care whether you believe me, she's real. I've seen her, several times. Her name is Mizuki."

The woman turned back to the man and snorted. "Ah yes, the infamous Mizuki. We'll just go out there now and grab her, huh? Our bad, we didn't mean to get you mixed up in all this." Sarcasm dripped from her words, but I was too tired to care. I could barely sleep, and over the last few days had gotten perhaps a few hours at best. It was all part of their tactics. Keep me tired. Keep me exhausted. Wear me down until I finally gave in and confessed, regardless of whether I did it or not.

Not to mention the buzz. Always the buzz... Rattling around in my ears like a bee unable to escape...

"She's going to kill again, you know. You're going to look real stupid then." I had no doubt in my mind. She could have already killed again, and I just didn't know it. It wasn't like I got any news in lockup. Maybe they heard about another killing and were keeping it hush-hush and planned to pin that one on me as well. Nothing would have surprised me at that point. "Can I have some water?"

The woman nodded and a glass of water was brought in. "How long do you plan on playing this game with us? You know that we can keep you here as long as we like, right? If I'm not mistaken..." she flicked through the papers in the folder before her "...Mr Shinji, you don't have any next of kin, correct?"

I nodded and took a drink.

"Says here you ran away from home when you were only 13, yes?"

I nodded again.

"Why was that?"

"What's that got to do with anything?"

"Humour me."

I sighed and put the glass back on the table. "My

father was a piece of shit. My mother was never home. There was no food in the house and my parents didn't notice when I didn't return for several days at a time. So I left. Simple as that."

"So you came from an abusive home? What do your parents do now?"

I shrugged. "How the hell should I know? I haven't heard from them in over 20 years."

She pursed her lips. "No girlfriends? Children?"

"Absolutely and entirely single." Her tone was getting on my nerves. Each tidbit she paraded in front of me was like how I had failed as a person in her eyes.

"Don't you get lonely?"

I laughed. "I'm a host. Lonely is the last thing I get."

"That's right, you are a host. And so were all the men who you killed. Rivals, correct?"

I placed my head back on the table. Back to the beginning of the vicious circle again. Several more hours of this were awaiting me, I knew it. They could swap out, change shifts, bring new people in, but I had to sit there in that tiny, dark room all day, for who knew how many hours, until finally it was time for bed. Then it began. The cleaning outside my cell. The officer rattling the bars with his baton. The testing of sirens. Loud white noise from the TV. Anything and everything that could make noise. You name it, that made sure it kept me from sleeping.

I would not crack. I was telling the truth. No matter what they threw at me, I would endure it. Before long, someone would realise I was missing, and it might not be my family, but I had friends and colleagues, even customers who would notice I was missing after a while. Sure, Club Tenshi was closed, but it wouldn't be closed forever. I just had to hold out.

Hold out...

That woman haunted my dreams. She was around every corner, in every window, behind every bush, and at the top of every set of stairs. A strong metallic smell followed her, and that laughter echoed wherever I went. Only when I looked down, it was me covered in blood, not her. She was stabbing the knife into the man's chest, she was cutting his face and destroying his livelihood, but it was me covered in blood.

It was me.

I screamed and sat up in bed. Outside the cell was dark minus a flickering light at the end of the hall. "Hello?" I called out. No response. I climbed to my feet and stuck my face against the bars, trying to see out. "Hello?" Still nothing.

Something clicked. I pushed and realised the door to my cell was open. "What the..." Hesitantly, I opened it further, and then stepped out into the hall. The cell across from mine was empty, and there was no officer in sight.

"Oh shi—"

That answered one question. I stumbled backwards, hitting the wall. The officer on duty was lying in a puddle of his own blood at the end of the hall, before the emergency exit. The light flickered above him, the only sound in the otherwise silent cells. *She* stood above him, her coat and mask bloodied. I wanted to scream, but couldn't find my voice. The knife in her hand clattered to the floor, and she turned heel and disappeared out the door.

What the hell? What was I supposed to do? It wouldn't be long until someone came to see why the officer was taking so long. They would find him dead, and me the only person around. My cell was unlocked. They wouldn't need my confession at that point. Several dead hosts were one thing, but a dead officer inside the precinct was another thing entirely. They would want blood, and they would get it.

There was no turning back. I couldn't hang around and wait for them to find me. There was no time to question what was going on. I ran past the man, pushed through the door, and emerged into the night.

31

MY LIFE WAS OVER. NO matter how you looked at it, this was it. I could never go back. The police already thought I was responsible for the death of several hosts inside Rakucho, and soon they were about to find the body of a dead officer, my cell door wide open, and me not in it.

I was done for. There was no hiding from this. Perhaps a new name and a fresh start somewhere else was my only hope to continue, but Rakucho was my home. It was all I knew, and I didn't want to go anywhere else. Tightness pulled at my cheeks as I ran through the humid night air, and that persistent buzz that had haunted me for days without any alcohol to kill it poked around in my head.

A few minutes after fleeing the station I recognised my surroundings. They were just a few blocks from Rakucho. I could feel her calling me back into her warm embrace. All would be okay.

CHAPTER THIRTY-ONE

Somehow. I just had to get there.

…Tightness. Of course! I smiled, for a moment not even noticing the buzzing drilling around in my brain. The plastic surgeon! The small procedure he'd done to reverse the ageing on my face was a huge success, so there was no reason why he couldn't take that a few steps further and give me a new face entirely. A new face… I could also take on a new name, and it wasn't like I had any family to inform. I could start over, a real new beginning. It would be like a personal challenge. See if I could rise to the top once more without any reputation or fame behind me. Just me and hard work. Perfect!

A woman laughed into her phone ahead of me. I snatched it from her hand without missing a stride and turned a corner. "Sorry, it's an emergency!" I screamed, not that it mattered. I hung up on whoever she was talking to and dialled the only number I knew off by heart; Yotchan. The clock in the corner said 3:13 a.m. There was no way that Yotchan would be asleep, this was prime work time for him. Yet the phone rang and rang. I hung up and hurled the phone into the bushes in disgust.

What could I do? I couldn't go home. I couldn't touch my bank accounts; not that anything was left in them, anyway. They would no doubt be all over the Club Tenshi workers, meaning Koji was out of the question.

That woman, Mizuki… she helped me. She let me out on purpose. I had to find her. I needed to find out why. Why was she doing this? Nothing made sense. My mind was a jumble, but if I could find her, that would be a good start.

"Excuse me, I'm looking for a woman in a trench coat." I grabbed a man exiting a nearby convenience store. "Long black hair, wears a face mask." The man tilted his head and sidestepped around me. I ran down the street and grabbed a woman walking with her friend. "Excuse me, I'm looking for—" She screamed and hit me with her bag and the pair ran off. I looked down. "Shit." I was still in the overalls the police gave me while they confiscated my clothes for evidence. I wasn't going to get anywhere like that.

Sirens blared in the distance. My heart dropped. They were looking for me. They'd found the officer and now they were looking for me. Whatever head start I had was about to vanish, and here I was, running around the streets in jail overalls. "Dammit!"

Rakucho. She was just a few blocks away, and something in my head was calling me there. An invisible lure that I couldn't and didn't want to resist. Rakucho was a big place, I could definitely hide there. But… where?

A man pushing a trolley staggered past on the other side of the street. I smiled. Of course. Tent Town. Not its official name, of course, but the northeast outskirts of Rakucho were filled with so many homeless that it was affectionately dubbed "Tent Town." Not so affectionately by those who lived and worked nearby, but not even the police bothered them anymore. There were simply too many, and the press didn't look good when police were seen beating or even killing homeless people in the capital. I could lie low there for a while until I figured out what to do. But first things first.

"Hey, buddy!" I jogged across the street and he stopped pushing his trolley. "Can you help a brother out? How much for the pants and jacket?"

He gave me the once over. "Whaddaya got?"

I had no pockets to keep money in. I had nothing. Nothing but the overalls on my back. "These? They're clean. Washed just last night."

The old man sniffed me and shrugged. "Ain't had clean for a while. Sure. Your loss." He removed his jacket, and I stripped in the street. "You running or something?" I said nothing. "Nothing to me if you are, just wanna know if I need to lie if asked about these."

"I—" I smiled. Rakucho always looked out for its own. "You didn't see me."

The old guy grinned. "Jokes on you because I actually can't." He tapped the side of his right eye. "This one's fully blind. But this one," he tapped the left, "still has a little life left in her. Not that anyone needs to know that." He winked. I handed him the overalls and yanked his pants up. Held together by a rope, nice. The old man took his time pulling the overalls up, and he was a good head shorter than me, so he looked like a child in them. A very old child. The sirens grew louder.

"Sounds like your friends are on their way, son. Never did like those guys." He tapped his eye again. "They're why I can't see."

"I'm sorry…"

"Pfft. I'm on my last legs, anyway. Go, young man, get out of here while you still can."

Young man. I grinned. It soon faded as the sirens

approached our direction. "Thank you," I said, patting him on the shoulder. "Really."

"Yeah, yeah. I don't even know who you are. Can't see anything. Some punk robbed me and I found these. Get outta here."

I patted his shoulder again and took off running through the bushes. Just a few short blocks away I'd find Tent Town. There I could take my time to gather my thoughts and plan my next move. Maybe someone there knew something about the trench coat woman as well.

32

LANTERNS LINED THE OUTSIDE OF Tent Town like a fence. Late-night revellers paid no attention as they stumbled by, laughing and holding each other up. Tent Town was just another part of Rakucho, and like the back of your hand, it was something you always saw but paid little attention to. Nobody noticed as I slipped inside.

The majority of the inhabitants were still awake. They were nocturnal creatures, much like Rakucho herself. Some guys sat around a lantern playing cards, while others played mahjong. One guy was tinkering with a piece of electronics, while another was reading a catalogue for a nearby department store. Most, however, sat by themselves, a drink in hand and head hidden from the world.

"Hey, uh, hi." I approached one man who was sitting in his beat-up foldable chair and staring off into space. He looked me up and down and grunted.

"Yeah?"

"I was hoping I could ask you a question."

"I ain't ya keeper."

I sat down on the tarp next to him. "Yeah, no, sure. Look, I'm looking for a woman."

The man laughed out loud, drawing several pairs of eyes in our direction. "You're in the wrong place, mate."

"No, not like that!" The eyes went back to their games and hobbies. "A woman in a trench coat. Have you seen or heard anything about her?"

"Trench coat, huh?" The man took a swig from his drink, and it hit me how long it had been since I'd had one. The sweet, sweet liquid that dulled the incessant buzz. I swallowed, my throat dry. He must have noticed, because he stopped for a moment before handing it to me. He leaned over and pulled out a fresh bottle for himself. "Bit hot for that, ain't it?"

I let the familiar bitterness wash down my parched throat and sighed in relief. "Yes, exactly. That's why I was hoping maybe someone had seen her."

"The trench coat woman?" A face appeared from behind the man's chair. An even older man crawled out and sat between us. He grabbed the bottle from my hand and took a drink himself. "I seen her."

"You have? Where? When?" Finally, a lead!

"A few streets from here. Must have been, oh, a few nights ago, perhaps. I didn't believe it at first, you know. I heard others talking about her. They said she ain't human. She be a monster, and that's why she gotta wear the mask. It hides all her teeth or something, I dunno. If she got all those teeth, why she gotta use a knife then, huh? She's clearly human."

I snatched the bottle back from him and drank as much as I could. When I was done, I planted the bottle on the ground and looked him in the eye. "Have you seen her recently? Tonight, maybe?"

He shook his head, but then pointed to one of the guys playing cards. There was a large cut on his face, covered with a bandage. "Hey, Hiro! Get over here!" The man put his cards down and as he approached, I saw he was quite young. Younger than me, even. "This guy wants to know about that monster lady y'all been talking about. What's her name?"

"Mizuki," I blurted out at the same time the young man replied, "Kuchisake."

"Mi-what?"

"Nothing. What did you call her?"

"...Kuchisake."

"Why do you call her that?"

He looked at me a few moments before glancing at his friends, as if to say, "Is this guy okay?"

"Well, her mouth has been cut pretty badly. So, you know. Kuchisake. Cut mouth."

Cut mouth. Yes. The tips of what appeared to be a massive mouth peeking out from beneath of her face mask. I'd seen it, several times. The grin as she killed the host right in front of my eyes before I hit the pavement came flooding back. I closed my eyes and shook my head. "Kuchisake. Yes. Fitting. Much better than what I was calling her."

"And what was that?"

"The trench coat woman. Doesn't really have the

same ring, does it?" The young man raised an eyebrow. "Anyway, what do you know about her? This... Kuchisake."

He shrugged. "Just rumours. Some say that she was jilted by a lover and now she's taking revenge. Others say she's looking for someone, and she's going to keep killing until she finds them. I heard some guys saying they heard one of the colour gangs murdered a woman and now she's back for revenge. That doesn't seem very likely though, because she's never touched any of them. We only know one thing about her."

"And what's that?"

He pointed to the cut on his face. "She has no interest in us. Only hosts."

I scratched the back of my head. In my hobo clothes and without any styling, there was no way for any of them to know I was a host. "What makes you say that?"

He gave a derisive laugh. "Because I'm the only person she let go. That we know of, anyway."

Oh. "Did she... do that..." I pointed to his face, unsure of the most polite way to ask how his face got maimed. He touched it again unconsciously.

"I was walking down the road, must have been around 2 or 3 in the morning, when suddenly someone grabbed me from behind. Before I knew what was going on she had a knife pressed to my cheek. I threw my hands up and looked up at her, and there was this flash in her eyes. I dunno how to describe it. It was like... I wasn't who she was after. She became an entirely different person."

"Then what happened?" I was on the edge of my

seat. This was more than I'd heard about her since I first learnt she was out there killing hosts in the city I loved. The city that raised me.

"Then I ran. She just let me go. I didn't hang around to ask her questions. What are you, slow?"

"Some people might say that." So, she grabbed this young man from behind, perhaps thinking him a host, and when she realised he wasn't, she let him go. Not before she'd already cut him, but as soon as she realised, she let him go. He'd seen her, and she didn't care. She only wanted hosts.

It still didn't make sense. What was her motive? What was the connection?

"Why are you so interested in her?" The young man's voice drew me back.

"Oh, uh, nothing really. I just need to find her. She... she killed someone I know." I waited for Jo or Haruki to make their grand entrance. Make all the homeless people think I was crazy. They'd been oddly quiet since the police picked me up. But they remained silent. It was almost lonely without them.

A few bugs buzzed around the nearby streetlight. Tent Town was tucked into the northeast corner of Rakucho, once a park but now home to those who had no place else to go. Tall buildings rose all around, exerting pressure on those below. Dark alleys snaked in all directions, threatening danger from all angles. And yet, this was probably the safest part of the entire city. Not from the police or the colour gangs or the yakuza, but from *her*.

My eyes closed of their own volition. I could no longer hear sirens. Wherever they were, it wasn't here.

"Anyway, I'm gonna get back to my cards." The young man lowered his head a little and walked off. The old guy next to me pulled another bottle of liquor out of god knows where and smiled.

"Drink?"

"Of course."

Within three minutes exhaustion caught up to me and I was fast asleep.

33

LOUD NOISES PULLED ME FROM my nightmarish sleep. For a moment I didn't know where I was, or what was happening, but it didn't take long for everything to fall into place. I was in Tent Town, on the run from the police, and some colours were rifling through the tent right behind me. It was still dark, but light filtered in from the streetlights and lanterns outside.

Yellows. Three of them. They didn't seem to have noticed me in the corner yet, but I recognised them. They were the same punks I'd caught trying to break into Club Tenshi. Now they were robbing the homeless. They really had no shame.

"What do you think you're doing?" The three of them turned towards me in an instant, the leader with his knife raised. Always with that pathetic little pocket knife. "Don't you have better things to be doing, like chasing down children in the park or something?"

"Who the fuck are you?"

My head buzzed so loudly I could barely hear them over the top of it. Whether it was a hangover, exhaustion, stress, or who knows what, it didn't matter; my head felt like it was going to explode.

I moved forward into the light so they could see me. "We've met before." They glanced at each other and shrugged. "You were trying to break into my club." Again they shrugged.

"I'm glad we're like, famous and shit, but I have no idea who the fuck you are."

Why wouldn't the buzz shut up? It was so loud. I shook my head. "Shut up…"

"…I don't think this guy's quite right in the head."

"You're telling me…"

"Get out of here before I—"

"Before what, hobo? You gonna tell the cops on us? Tell them we stole your, what? Your tent? Because you ain't got much else here for a homeless guy. Slim pickings, even for someone like you."

"I'm not…"

"…Not what?"

My head felt like it was going to explode. I grabbed the kid's wrist and smashed it with my other hand, making him drop the knife. He fell to his knees while his buddies jumped on me. Fists connected with my face and shoulders while kicks assailed my body. I curled up, the only thing I could think to do in the moment, and wait for my head to paint the tent red.

The kid picked up the knife and jabbed it at me. I

moved my head, but pain quickly tore through my cheek. Warm blood trickled down my face and onto the dirt below.

"Aww, shit man, you cut him!"

"What the hell do you think I have this knife for?"

"You didn't say we were gonna cut 'em!"

"Then he shouldn't have started shit!"

"We gotta get outta here, man. Before he calls his friends!"

"You mean the hobos outside? They saw us come in. They know. And they still turned a blind eye because they don't wanna be next."

I grabbed my cheek and blood poured out between my fingers. My face. They cut my face. I opened my mouth and fresh pain tore through me, matching the screaming in the back of my head. I tentatively touched it with my tongue and felt my fingers. I almost threw up.

They cut my face. Right through my cheek. Just like her. Just like Kuchisake. I would have laughed if I wasn't in so much pain. It was all over. Even if they didn't kill me, I had nothing left now. Surgery couldn't save this. My image, my livelihood, all gone. All because of a couple of kids in yellow tracksuits.

I screamed and lunged for the boy. He dropped the knife as my bloody fingers closed around his throat. He had ended my career. My future. All the plans I had, everything I was working so hard towards, all gone now. Nobody would want to spend time with a disfigured host, and no amount of surgery would be able to fix it. There would be no name change, no facial reconstructions to make me look like a new man. The police were after me. I had nowhere to go. The only option left remaining now torn out from underneath me. All because of this little punk. I squeezed harder, waiting to feel something crush beneath my fingers.

This was all Haruki's fault. If he hadn't come in, then none of this would have happened. Everything was great and dandy until he showed up. I could have retired in a year or two on my own terms and lived out the rest of my life in luxury. But the moment he came into town, everything went to shit. I saw his face beneath me, blood dripping on his cheeks, and I smiled. Pain spread through my cheek like fire, but that just made me smile even more. It fed the anger channelling down through my forearms and into this punk's neck. He did this. He ruined my life. He deserves it. Cause and effect. He brought this upon himself.

But he wasn't alone. It was also Jo's fault. That tiny, bald, muscular man that looked more like a Buddhist monk than a host. He put no effort into learning fashion, he spent no money on his non-existent hair, and he spent his free time bulking up instead of taking ladies on after-hours dates, yet he still he overtook me. Then he had the audacity to keep hanging around after death, like I had something to do with it! He was the one who deserved it, not me! What effort had he ever put into the job? What sacrifices had he ever made in his efforts to become the best? None! He deserved what he got! Not me! This was all—

Something hit the back of my head and sent me

sprawling to the ground. Coughing, the kid grabbed his knife and held it towards me with a shaky hand. "Y-You're fucking insane." He coughed a few more times and shoved his friends out of the tent. "I'll remember this. We ever meet again, y-you're dead."

Black dots swam in front of my eyes and a drill bored into the back of my head. People were moving outside. They'd be coming to see what all the fuss was about soon. I pushed myself to my feet and wiped the other side of my face with the blood on my hands. "N-Not if I get you first."

"Come on, let's get outta here!" one of the kid's friends said. He kept the knife pointed at me a few more moments before he turned and took off, disappearing into the night. Murmurs rose outside. I pushed my way through the back of the tent and staggered onto the grass. They'd find what looked like a murder scene inside with no body. Perhaps that was for the best.

Rakucho welcomed me back into her bosom with open arms. Blood dripped from my cut face as I stumbled down a dark alley.

It was over. Everything. It was all over.

34

A VOICE BROKE THROUGH THE buzz. "We told you."

I swiped at the side of my face. Nothing was there. Nothing but pain and blood. My feet pounded the pavement below, carrying me to who knows where. Unfortunately, some unwanted friends were along for the ride as well. They were back.

"You're just like us now." Haruki's voice, whispering to my right.

"Leave me alone!"

"Even if we wanted to, we can't," Jo's voice, whispering to my left.

"I said, leave me alone! This is all your fault!"

"You're stuck with us, and we with you. Although, it would appear that you'll soon be joining us on this side as well. Pity. You were more fun to play with alive."

I closed my eyes and kept running. Maybe I could outrun them. My head swam and sickness rose in my stomach. Stopping by the side of the road, I let the meagre contents of my stomach out and screamed in pain. A voice laughed. Tears rolled down my cheeks.

"It's nothing less than you deserve after all. You did this to us."

Enough of this. "Did what? What did I do to you? You did this to me!" I got back to my feet, knees shaking and screaming at the air. "You keep saying I did this! Did what? Tell me! I'd love to know!

Jo's face materialised out of the bushes. His jaw lolled and blood oozed out of the wounds in his chest. Dirt and leaves matted to the blood all over him, but his body below the chest tapered off into nothing. He floated before me, a grotesque mockery of a bust doing his best to keep his jaw on.

"She killed us because of you. You did it. As good as if it were your own hand."

That really didn't make any sense. Haruki appeared behind him. I averted my gaze. I couldn't stand to look at either of them.

"I'd still be alive if it weren't for you. If you'd just retired when you were supposed to."

"Supposed to? I wasn't aware that there was an expiration date on my career! On my life!" Their baseless accusations fuelled my anger, which was already burning on the fumes of my pain. "I wasn't the one who killed you! I don't even know who that woman is!"

"But you do."

I stopped, my mouth open mid-retort. Did they mean Mizuki? Sure, I knew her name, but only because Koji told me. I had no memory of who the woman actually was. By that logic, I knew every single person in Rakucho, and then some. I had no idea how old she was, what she did, where she lived, how long she'd been coming to Rakucho, how long she'd been coming to Club Tenshi, what her hobbies were, if she had family, what her favourite animal was. Nothing. All I knew was a name that the club bartender had given me. I knew my neighbour who kept leaving cigarette butts by my doorstep better than that, and I didn't even know his name! But at least I knew where he lived, and what he looked like.

Haruki moved to the side, making his way behind me. Something felt wrong. Something felt terribly, terribly wrong.

I ran, blind of where my feet were taking me. The deeper that Rakucho pulled me in, the more despair I felt. I would never work here again. Never walk her night streets with a beautiful lady on my arm, her money paying for the night's entertainment before I took her home for a little after-hours fun. I would never again see my face lighting up the billboard at the end of the main street, my glistening smile beaming down upon all who entered. The memories of my youth on the streets, my struggle to become number one, everything that I had ever experienced in Rakucho… It had all come to an end. At the end of some nameless punk's knife.

My heart pounded erratically and I stopped. Was it the adrenaline, the exhaustion… or the woman standing before me? The woman in the trench coat and blood-speckled face mask. The woman they called the Rakucho Nightcrawler. The trench coat woman. Kuchisake.

Mizuki.

"Just do it," I said, my breathing laboured. The pain in my cheek was unbearable, and perhaps ironically, after all that, it was a kid from a colour gang who ruined my life and not her. If her goal all this time was to set me up and then destroy my life, she could have gone about it much quicker and easier. *He* had. Now, I had nothing left. What good was I without my looks? All that work I put in, and for nought. "Go on, just kill me. You'd be doing me a favour."

She said nothing. Her silence made my blood boil.

"Come on!" I screamed, sending fresh waves of pain shooting up through my face. My legs teetered, and I put a hand against the streetlight to keep myself upright. She stood in the distance beneath the next one, the light shining down on her like a cruel message from above. Here is your saviour. Sorry she's a little violent, but cruel gods do like to play cruel tricks. She made no signs of movement. Just watched me in silence, frozen to the spot.

I strode towards her, trying to appear as threatening as my wobbly legs would make me. The buzzing in my head, the throbbing in my cheek, the pain boring into the back of my eyes; it was all too much. I just wanted it to end. Bring the bliss of silence, of nothingness, down upon me. End it. I had nothing to live for anymore and I certainly didn't want to spend the rest of my life like this. "Do it!" I screamed as I got closer. She didn't flinch, nor move a muscle. She held her ground, hands in her pockets, and her eyes watched with interest as I approached.

I stood before her, toe to toe. "This is what you wanted, isn't it?" I said, pointing to my face. Her eyes flickered to my cheek for the first time and something unexpected ran through them; regret? Her brow furrowed, just for an instant, and then the usual veneer of amusement returned.

"Why did you do it?" My voice cracked, but I grabbed her by the shoulders and shook. What did I care if she pulled out her knife and started stabbing me like she had the others? On the contrary, that would finally put me out of my misery! I would welcome it! I would take her knife and do it myself if she didn't have the guts to! How's that for a retirement?

Instead, she reached up and removed her mask, revealing for the first time just what was hiding beneath it.

35

SO IT WAS TRUE. I'D seen hints of it, nightmarish glimpses of what appeared to be a mouth far too large to be normal; of cuts that marred her face in a grotesque, inhuman fashion. Not scars, but an open mouth that didn't seem to know where to end, revealing all of the teeth inside, right to the back of her jaw. But they were just that; glimpses. Easy to dismiss as the alcohol speaking, or the stress of the situation. People loved rumours, and the more horrifying the better. Of course they called her Kuchisake. Everyone loved a good monster.

Yet here she was. Standing before me. As real as the pain in my face and the buzz in the back of my head.

Up close I could see just how far her mouth was cut. The edges extended all the way up to below her ears, cut jagged and rough like it had been hacked with a blunt saw. The scarring was intensive, but it hadn't healed her wounds at all. When she smiled, it spread all the way up her face. Every single one of her teeth were visible, right up to the back.

"Do you think I'm pretty?"

It took a few moments to register that she'd spoken to me. I suddenly laughed in her face, unable to stop myself at such an unexpected question. After I regained my composure, I leaned closer and looked deep into her eyes, searching for the truth.

"Am I?"

Then it hit me. Those eyes. I did know them. I leaned back a moment and took the rest of her in. Even setting aside the cuts marring her cheeks, I didn't recognise anything else about her, but I knew those eyes. Somewhere, something in the back of my mind was going off like a bell. I had definitely seen this woman somewhere before, but where? When?

"Mizuki?" I tested her name, the sound foreign on my lips. Something flashed through her eyes before she set her jaw again. Seeing it happen through the gaping hole in her cheek was unsettling to say the least.

"Now do you remember?"

"Remember...?" She pressed something into my hand. When I opened it, there was a red spider lily looking back at me. "Oh..."

Memories came flooding back. She smiled as she saw the cogs turning. I was never any good with names. I was slightly better with faces, although there were times where I got called out for not remembering someone who felt that I should have. But, I was real good at remembering the key traits of customers, and associating something with them so when I saw them again, I could bring that up and they would feel important. Remembered. This was the key factor in bringing back repeat customers. Everybody wanted to feel loved. Everybody wanted to be remembered.

The flower. Of course. Only one customer had ever presented me with a red spider lily throughout the 20 years of my career. It was such a strange, unique gesture that I never forgot it. The flower of death. It wasn't something you forgot a customer giving you so easily.

"You look… different." I didn't know how else to put it.

She had first come to see me a year earlier, although she looked nothing like she did now. She was a little chubbier then, her nose wider, cheeks rounder, and lips thinner. Entirely unremarkable… other than the red spider lily she always carried around. She spent a lot of money on me at first, and every time I saw that red spider lily I knew that money was coming in. She wasn't a looker, but she had money. That was all that mattered. She presented me with the flower at the end of our first meeting and it had both fascinated and creeped me out. Then she stopped coming in after a while and I never saw her again.

The woman standing in front of me had her eyes, but the rest of her was completely different. "What happened to—"

She placed a hand on my cut cheek and I grunted in pain. Then she tapped the back of my ear. "You hear it too, don't you?"

What? No way. She couldn't... I widened my eyes. "Hear what?"

"It gets worse when it's quiet. It makes you angry. Drives you insane. The buzz."

I grabbed her shoulders before I could stop myself. "Yes! What is it! How do I make it stop?"

She smiled. It sent a jolt of terror down my spine, but I held her shoulders tight. "You saw Dr Nakata as well, huh?"

"...Dr Nakata?" The surgeon from Smiling Bright? "*He* did this?"

"I went for my first visit six months ago. Free of charge. If I liked what he did..."

"...Then you could come back for more." Just like he had said to me. She nodded. When she wasn't grinning, she almost looked normal. Almost. The gaping holes in the side of her face were still kind of terrifying.

"I just wanted to look a little nicer. Make my nose a little smaller, get rid of some of the fat in my cheeks. Look beautiful, like everyone else. But I didn't have much money left by that point. I spent most of it on you."

I didn't know what to say.

"After the first operation, there was a constant buzz. I thought maybe something went wrong. I went back. He said that was normal. We proceeded with the second operation. The buzz got worse."

"...What happened then?"

She pointed to her cheeks. "After a while, it spread. I could feel it in my teeth. I wanted it to end. I wanted it all to end."

I swallowed. She did that to herself? What type

of person could…

Her jaw set again, and she smiled. It was just as horrifying as the first time. "So. Do you think I'm pretty? I did this for you, after all. All of this was for you."

"…You did what?" I understood the words, but not the intent behind them. It was like the words hit a brick wall in front of my face and I saw them, but they weren't getting through.

"You've been struggling too, haven't you?"

"Struggling?"

"Younger hosts coming in. Taking your money. Taking your position."

I took a step back.

"You were always my favourite, Narumi. I told you I'd always look out for you. Remember?"

The red spider lily seemed to drip with blood from my hand. Maybe it was.

"How is this… I never asked you to…" I couldn't form a complete sentence. I couldn't form a complete thought. My brain was running a thousand miles a minute and, if I were to be completely honest, the lack of blood was starting to win out over adrenaline and making me woozy. The wound on my cheek had started to crust over, but it was painful unlike anything I could have ever imagined. And she did that to herself? To stop the buzz? "No…"

"You are Rakucho's rightful number one, Narumi. You were the only man to ever give me the time of day. To make me feel special. They don't deserve that spot. You do."

"No… You didn't… I didn't ask…" I held my

head. The buzz grew stronger, louder, like my head was about to burst right off my shoulders.

"Rakucho is full of people like them," she continued. "They care for nothing but themselves. I've watched them. I've seen them. I know what they're like. They use people and abuse them and leave them nothing but a hollow shell of their former selves."

As she grew more impassioned, it was difficult to think she was talking of anything other than herself.

"But not you, Narumi. I tried to join their world, and even got surgery to look beautiful like them, but it did nothing! They still wouldn't give me the time of day. You were the only one, Narumi. Even before all of..." she gestured to her face "...this. And now look at what they've done to you. They tried to push you out. They made fun of your age, your looks. They pushed you to get surgery, just like me. It wouldn't have made a difference, Narumi. They would have joked behind your back even more. 'Look at that guy, unable to let go. How sad. How pathetic.' But that's not you."

"You don't even know me!"

She laughed. She pulled the knife out of her coat and held it before her. I stepped back before I could stop myself. "But I do, Narumi. You're not without your flaws, but you're not like them. They were going to eat you up and toss you out, just like they did to me. I couldn't allow that to happen. You weren't the one who deserved to go. They were."

I pointed to my face, anger flaring up once more. "What good does that matter? Look at this! Look at it! I'll never work here again. Nobody is going to pay money to spend time with me now! My life is ruined! There's nothing left for me anymore…"

She stepped forward, and I took another step back. The smile on her face did the opposite of setting me at ease, but in my other hand she placed the knife.

"Sure there is. There's still one more left."

One more?

Then it hit me.

I grinned.

36

THE WOODEN HANDLE OF THE knife felt cool in my hand. Soothing. Right. I lifted the red spider lily to smell it, closing my eyes to take it in.

"Does the buzz ever go away?"

She shook her head.

"How did he do it? Why?"

She shook her head again. "His procedures are experimental. I think he knows exactly what he's doing."

"You're saying he did it on purpose?"

She nodded.

"He's... making people like you?" I stopped and corrected myself. "Like us?"

She shrugged.

"Why?"

"Does he need a reason? Some people just enjoy the suffering of others. They're evil. All the way to the core."

I saw myself plunging the knife into his chest.

Over and over. Carving a giant smile on his face so that when they found his body, they would see the grotesque mockery he had made of others had found its way home to him. Smiling Bright. It was right there in the surgery name. I laughed in disgust.

Mizuki held up something in her other hand. Her bloodied mask. "They're looking for you." Oh yeah. The police. I grabbed it and held it with the red spider lily.

"Why do you like this flower so much?"

She smiled. "The red spider lily is so resilient that it grows even in Hell. Paths of them guide people through the afterlife to be reborn once more. They're beautiful, don't you think?"

"Yeah... I guess." I couldn't say I'd ever thought about the meaning behind it before. It was just a creepy looking flower.

"I used to think that Rakucho was Hell on Earth. A den of sin that collected the worst of the worst. I was attacked by men the very first time I came here." The grin on her face was not gentle, and certainly not kind. "A handsome man saved me. Threw the attackers off, helped me up, and then went on his way once he was sure they were gone. I didn't get his name, but I found a red spider lily on the ground as he walked off. I picked it up, and as I was wandering around Rakucho in a daze, I came across a sign. There he was. My saviour, right in the middle."

She looked down lovingly at the flower and closed my fist around it. I had no memory of what she was talking about, but then again, such sights weren't uncommon in Rakucho either. I'd helped numerous men and women over the years.

"Rakucho is rotten," she continued. "It's true. It is Hell on Earth. But not all of it is rotten. Sometimes even a flower can grow. And that flower can help guide lost souls to somewhere better. Somewhere they deserve to be."

Somewhere they deserved to be. I grinned.

"You're very pretty."

"...What?" For the first time, she looked taken aback.

"You asked me if I think you're pretty. Yes. You're very pretty." I put the mask on. Behind the bloodied mask and in the hobo's dirty jacket and pants I looked nothing like the Shinji Narumi of old. With the knife in hand, I felt a power like none I'd ever experienced before. Was this what she felt? Hidden behind her coat and mask, her face completely different to the one those who knew her remembered, and with the power of life and death in her hand. That power was intoxicating.

The buzz was loud and persistent, but in that moment it didn't bother me. Nor did I hear the voices of Jo and Haruki. They were gone. Completely gone. Afraid of *her*.

Maybe my life wasn't over. Maybe I had been looking at everything the wrong way, and it had taken this single red flower to guide me back on course. Just like it had her.

Rakucho. My mother. The only thing that had ever provided for me, cared for me, looked after me my whole life. She was being overrun by filth. The colour gangs were once again bloodying her name. Surgeons were sullying her children. The police turned the other way, unwilling to dirty their own hands and hoping that when they opened their tightly clenched eyes, everything would have fixed itself. But that wasn't how things worked. You couldn't just turn a blind eye and hope for the best.

Life finds a way to balance itself out. I heard that somewhere once. Rakucho had lost her balance. No, it had been forcibly ripped from her. She had raised me since I was a lost child, and as an adult I had strayed too far and lost my way again. She was guiding me back, giving me purpose. The police wouldn't save her. The gangs would continue to grow. Then the yakuza would move back in to assert their dominance and there would be wars. Murders of innocents would rise, people would fear entering her limits, and before long the police would be forced to move in. Policies would be passed, measures taken, and the Rakucho I knew and loved would be gone.

At heart, she was a good city. One of the few places that accepted who you were, no matter what, and my ambition to stay at the top had blinded me to the changes that had been taking place for years. Not just recently; years. The colour gangs were just the newest of the fleas on the dog's back, and while they were currently the noisiest, they weren't the only infestation.

Mizuki looked up at me in silence. "You're very pretty," I said. I gripped the knife tighter. "And you're right. We've got work to do."

Rakucho would return to her former glory, once all the fleas were picked off. The time for the colours was coming. They were too loud. Too noisy. Drew too much attention. It was time for them to retire from Rakucho's streets once more. But before them, there was someone much more important to take care of. Someone who was working behind the scenes. Someone who hid in the shadows, quietly ruining lives right in plain sight.

It was time to pay a visit to Smiling Bright.

WANT EVEN MORE?

Also available in *The Torihada Files*:
Kage
Jukai

Toshiden: Exploring Japanese Urban Legends
Volume One
Volume Two

Reikan: The most haunted locations in Japan

Kowabana: 'True' Japanese scary stories from around the internet:
Volume One
Volume Two
Volume Three
Origins
Volume Five

Read new stories each week at Kowabana.net, or get them delivered straight to your ear-buds with the *Kowabana* podcast!

ABOUT THE AUTHOR

Tara A. Devlin studied Japanese at the University of Queensland before moving to Japan in 2005. She lived in Matsue, the birthplace of Japanese ghost stories, for 10 years, where her love for Japanese horror really grew. And with Izumo, the birthplace of Japanese mythology, just a stone's throw away, she was never too far from the mysterious. You can find her collection of horror and fantasy writings at taraadevlin.com and translations of Japanese horror at kowabana.net.

Made in the USA
Las Vegas, NV
12 January 2022